The Handsome Enemy

Emily Walters

The Handsome Enemy

Published by Emily Walters

Copyright © 2019 by Emily Walters

ISBN 978-1-07053-524-1

First printing, 2019

All rights reserved. No part of this book may be reproduced in any form or by any electronic or mechanical means including information storage and retrieval systems – except in the case of brief quotations in articles or reviews – without the permission in writing from its publisher, Emily Walters.

www.EmilyWaltersBooks.com

PRINTED IN THE UNITED STATES OF AMERICA

Dedication

I want to dedicate this book to my beloved husband, who makes every day in my life worthwhile. Thank you for believing in me when nobody else does, giving me encouragement when I need it the most, and loving me simply for being myself.

Table of Contents

CHAPTER 1 1

CHAPTER 2 10

CHAPTER 3 16

CHAPTER 4 22

CHAPTER 5 30

CHAPTER 6 38

CHAPTER 7 50

CHAPTER 8 64

CHAPTER 9 75

CHAPTER 10 82

CHAPTER 11 95

CHAPTER 12 102

CHAPTER 13 109

CHAPTER 14 115

EPILOGUE 120

WHAT TO READ NEXT? 122

ABOUT EMILY WALTERS 125

ONE LAST THING... .... **126**

Chapter 1

Reagan Lister looked up at the knock on her door and smiled, seeing her boss, Martin Fitz, at the open doorway. "Hey Martin, come on in."

The older man walked in and took a seat in one of the chairs in front of her oak desk, unbuttoning his suit coat in the process. Martin Fitz was the anchor of Fitz & Associates, a swanky law firm on the Upper East Side of Manhattan. Reagan had been working for him for two years, her first job after passing the bar, and hadn't regretted taking the job. In the two years she had been here, Martin had helped her become the lawyer she was today.

"Reagan," he started, giving her a grin. "What are you working on so hard?"

"I've got that massive case that has just been placed on the docket," she answered with a sigh. "The Kilner case." After jumping through all the hoops of the grand jury and indictment phases, the case was finally ready to go to trial, which meant a significant amount of work on her part. She was ready though.

"Big case," he agreed with a nod of his head. "That's what I want to talk to you about."

Reagan sat up straighter in her chair, surprised. He had given her the case months ago, a very high-profile case that involved the killing of a young woman after a wild party in a ritzy penthouse belonging to a senator's son. The media was all over this one and while the senator's son insisted that he was innocent, the public was ready to lock him up and throw away the key without trial. Right now, the client was holed up in his family's estate in the Hamptons, out on a significant amount of bail while he waited for his trial. Reagan was the one representing him and she was due to meet with her client in a few days for prep. The trial itself wouldn't take place until the end of the month. "What's up?"

Martin rubbed his balding head with his hand. "I'm worried about this one, Reagan. I'm not going to lie to you. There is a lot of pressure for us to prove his innocence. I have the mayor breathing down my neck on this one."

Reagan smiled sympathetically. "Don't worry, Martin. I'll make it happen." Though she wasn't quite sure how that was going to happen exactly. Ben Kilner had found the young woman in his penthouse by himself and instead of calling the police immediately, he made his first call to his father. That alone was enough to put doubt about his innocence in the minds of jurors. Coupled with the fact that the woman had been seen with Ben that night, Reagan knew she was going to be facing an uphill battle even though no murder weapon had been found. But she could do it. There was a smoking gun out there somewhere, she just had to find it.

"I'm bringing in some help," Martin blurted out a moment later. "Gregory Pilster."

"What?" Reagan said, shock in her voice. "Why would you do that?"

Martin had the grace to look uncomfortable as he looked at her. "I'm sorry, Reagan. I think you are a great lawyer and all. But this one, this case is going to be difficult even for you. Greg, he had that win in the Riley case last year. He's got experience."

"Whereas I do not," she answered for him, fury in her veins. How dare he not think she could do this?

"It's not that, Reagan," he answered defensively. "Greg is wanting to get out of solo practice. He graduated top of his class and has about three years on you regarding handling these types of trials, you know, the ones where your picture is plastered all over the news for weeks? You haven't gone through that type of pressure and scrutiny yet, Reagan, and I think you can stand to learn a lot from him."

"I graduated top of my class as well," Reagan replied coolly, crossing her arms over her chest as she stared at him. "I don't need a babysitter, Martin. I can do this."

Martin pushed himself out of his chair, a frown on his face. "I expect you to do this, Reagan," he said to her, the look on his face telling Reagan he wasn't going to change his mind. "Greg will be here tomorrow to help oversee this case. See that you brief him on everything you have so far. If we play our cards right, I might be able to get him to join the firm as a partner after all of this is said and done. He will be a valuable asset."

Reagan gritted her teeth as Martin walked out of her office, waiting until he left to put her head in her hands, fighting the urge to scream aloud. He was bringing in another lawyer. Not just any lawyer, but Gregory Pilster, a hotshot lawyer from Houston. She had heard of him alright, who hadn't? His name had been all over the news after the Riley case, a woman accused of killing her politician husband. Her stance was that she thought he was an intruder and though the evidence didn't exactly corroborate her story, Pilster still won the case. Reagan could still remember the shock that had reverberated throughout the country when the verdict had come down and the smiling defendant had been set free with her lawyer at her side, his grin letting everyone know that he had just scored a huge win. The case itself had been full of lies and deceit, the politician's dark past of strip clubs and drug money coming out during the trial more than once. The media ate it up and the case was definitely exciting enough to have everyone glued to the TV day after day as the trial was shown live.

Lifting her head, Reagan looked down at the file she was starting to build, some of her excitement deflating. Now she would be forced to share this case

The Handsome Enemy

with a colleague that loved the limelight and while she hadn't wanted to make this a media circus, as soon as they found out that Pilster was on the case, the media would be looking for every small tidbit. The handsome lawyer would draw them like a moth to a flame. Not only that, but Martin wanted to make him partner. Partner! That was what she had hoped for in a few years, when Martin would retire and she would step up. After all, she was the strongest in the firm, the other lawyers' success rates were nothing like hers was.

But with Pilster in the way, it would be another tough climb for her. She couldn't let it happen. She had worked too hard for this. No, Reagan would make Pilster's life miserable while he was here so that when it came time for this case to be over, he would run back to Texas in his cowboy boots.

***

The Next Day

Gregory Pilster stepped off the plane and pulled his coat tighter around him, already hating the colder weather of New York. When he had left Houston, it had been a nice seventy degrees, even in November. But here, he was looking at fifties. His warm blood couldn't adapt.

He found his luggage and walked toward the exit, his mind already on the case he had read while in the air.

This was his type of case, with political implications and so much media surrounding it that it was on everyone's lips, anticipation at a high buzz. This was what he needed. After dealing with the less sensational cases that he had over the last year, Greg couldn't wait to fall back into a high-profile one. After all, it was where he shined the most. It had been like fate when Fitz had come to see him last month in Houston, wanting him to come on up to New York and join his firm. "I have some good lawyers," he had said as they had talked over drinks that night. "But none are as good as you. I want you to come and mentor them, maybe even take over the practice for me someday. The money's good, I swear it."

And Fitz was right. The money was going to be real good, along with the nice apartment downtown he wasn't going to have to pay for during the time he worked on the case and the chance to be in New York, where big cases were a dime a dozen. No, Greg couldn't turn this down. So, he had leased his apartment in Houston and packed his bags.

Hailing a cab, Greg gave the directions to the firm and sat back, his mind already teeming with ideas for this case. First, he wanted to talk to the client, get a feel for whether they could win this thing. Based on the file that was sent to him, it looked like it could go either way with whether the accused was going to walk free or go to jail. Only time and good

The Handsome Enemy

preparation would tell which way the jury would decide this man's fate.

Grabbing the file out of his briefcase, Greg thought about the lawyer's name he had researched that he would be partnering with. Her headshot showed a pretty blonde who looked like she should still be in college, not heading up such a high-profile case. She had graduated top of her class and by Martin's ravings, was on her way to becoming a great lawyer. But this wasn't her case. This was going to be his case. She would understand that he was far more experienced to handle this type of case and she would be the second in command during the trial. Everyone had to have the stepping-stones to this type of case and he was going to show her the ropes.

The cab arrived at a tall office building and Greg paid the guy before walking into the building and pressing the elevator button to go up. The door to the building flew open and the woman of his thoughts hurried in, tucking a strand of hair behind her ear as she came to stand beside him. She was tall, dressed in a pair of black pants and a blouse that showed off her thin frame. Her features were classic beauty, though her mouth was turned in a frown as she read the paper in her hands. "Really?" she muttered under her breath. "Who released that?"

He chuckled, unable to help it and she looked up, her eyes narrowing. "You."

The Handsome Enemy

Greg stuck out his hand, keeping his friendly grin. "Greg Pilster. Nice to meet you."

She looked down at his hand and her frown grew as her eyes traveled back up to his face. "I don't know what Martin told you, but I don't need help. I have this case handled."

He had to give it to her. She was holding her ground. "I'm here to assist. Think of me as a good sounding board."

"I have a board in my office," she said as the elevator doors opened. "Though I doubt I can throw push pins at you."

He burst out into laughter, thinking he had met media people that were friendlier than she was being right now. She stepped forward and her heel caught on the crack sending her pitching forward into the elevator. He reached out and grabbed her around the waist, hauling her back at the last moment against him, smelling the fruity scent of her hair as it tickled his nose. "Whoa," he said softly. "Do you know how many people die in elevators each year?"

"Let me go," she said, struggling against his tight hold. He released her and she stumbled forward, spinning around with her hands on her hips. "Don't ever touch me."

Greg crossed his arms over his chest, giving her a wry smile. "So, I should have let you fall flat on your face then?"

She huffed and pressed the button for the third floor, clearly done with him. He hurried to catch the ride, stepping inside just in time for the doors to shut behind him. Greg cleared his throat, amused that she already had this opinion of him coming to help with this case, no, own this case. He admired her spunk, but that was only going to get her so far. She needed grit, determination, and some experience, all of which he had.

"This is not your case, it's mine."

Turning, he looked at her rigid pose, the way she was staring ahead though her jaw was clenched tightly. "What?"

She turned to him then and he could see the fire in her eyes. "I said this is my case. I don't care what Martin told you. I'm going to win it."

He gave her a nod. "We will see about that."

She didn't say anything as the doors opened and she stepped out of the elevator. Greg followed her. The gauntlet had been thrown apparently.

Chapter 2

"What a jerk," Reagan muttered to herself as she walked through the office, knowing that this Pilster guy was behind her, following her. She had already had a bad morning to begin with. Her alarm clock hadn't gone off and luckily she had awoken to see that she was indeed late to work. Then, as she grabbed a seat on the subway for her ride into work, she logged into her emails from her laptop to find out that her client had decided to go on one of the nightly news shows in two days to tell his side of the story. That was not in the plans and Reagan was going to have to go talk to her client sooner than she had anticipated.

"Good morning," Martin said as she passed by his office, his eyes lighting up as he saw who was tagging along behind her. "Greg! You made it!"

"I did," Greg said smoothly, stopping to talk to Martin. Reagan kept on going to her own office, not wanting to hear anything else. The man was encroaching on her case and she couldn't stand the fact that Martin had brought someone else in to "help." After putting her bag on her desk, Reagan placed her hands on the wooden top and forced herself to take a breath. She had to pull it together. She was flustered and royally pissed off about all the events of this morning already, but it wasn't going to help her show Martin she could handle this professionally. So what if Pilster was here? She was going to treat him like a chair in the corner, like he didn't even exist.

Reagan pushed away from the desk and looked down the hall, where Pilster and her boss were still talking. She had to admit, the camera hadn't lied about his good looks. He was tall and broad-shouldered, with dark brown hair that was slicked back on his head and a short, dark beard. The blue suit fit his body very well and when he had kept her from falling flat on her face just minutes ago, she could feel the steely strength of him. In fact, her body had liked it all too well when he had pressed her against him. Her nerves were still in a frenzy from just that simple contact.

"Ugh, quit thinking about him," she groaned softly, falling into her chair and clicking on her computer. So what if he had been the first man to touch her with the exception of a handshake in two years? It didn't mean she didn't want to have an intimate relationship, but her work claimed most of her attention and she didn't have time to go out and make friends. It was a sad existence.

"Reagan," Martin said as he entered her office, a smile on his face. Pilster was right behind him, an easy smile on his handsome face. She scowled, crossing her arms over her chest. He thought this was going to be easy, but she had other ideas. "I'm going to have a temporary space set up in here for Greg. That way you and he can work closely together."

"I'm sure Mr. Pilster would like to have his own space," she said in rebuttal, not wanting to share her office. That would mean she would be forced to spend all her workdays with him. She needed space to prove she could do this, not a babysitter constantly looking over her shoulder!

"Oh, I'm fine with sharing," Pilster piped up, giving Martin a grin. "Besides, we will be working closely together anyway. This will eliminate any need to repeat information we learn."

Reagan huffed aloud, not caring that Martin's eyebrow raised at the sound. She wanted him to see her displeasure about this entire arrangement. "Fine. He can have my office. I'm not planning to be here anyway."

"Why is that?" Martin asked, both of his eyebrows rising now.

"I've got to go visit my client sooner than expected," she stated, thinking about the idiotic move her client was about to make. She knew why he wanted to. Garner public sympathy, get everyone on his side before trial. But she didn't like when clients did this without consulting her first. A client's lawyer should always be present, even if it wasn't on camera, so that the questions could be screened and answers already fabricated so that they said nothing to further incriminate themselves. Reagan figured that maybe her client's father was behind this public display, but there was going to be only one way to find out. "I'll be gone a couple days."

"Great, Greg will go with you then," Martin said, his tone telling her that she might as well not even bother fighting his decision. "It will give you a chance to get to know each other."

"But I was planning on staying a couple days," Reagan protested. There were a few bed and breakfasts near where her client was staying and she figured she would spend a day or two there, starting her prep early, once she talked him out of this interview. Reagan was really concerned about Ben and how he was going to handle being on the stand. Their previous talks hadn't gone so well and she wanted to spend extra time with her prep. This was a high-profile case and would be very stressful on them all in the next few weeks. He needed to focus on the trial, not this interview.

"Put it on the company account then," Martin answered, turning to walk out of the office. "Good luck."

Reagan held her tongue, knowing she was fighting a losing battle. Martin wanted them to go together.

"Well," Pilster said, looking around her office. "Maybe we should start over again. I'm Greg. I'm not your enemy, Reagan."

"Listen," she interrupted, looking him in the eye so he could see that she wasn't going to back down. She wasn't intimidated by his expertise. "This is my case. If we are going to be forced to work together, there are some rules."

"Rules," Greg repeated, a slight smirk coming over his face. "Alright, what are they?"

Reagan bit the inside of her cheek to keep from saying something she shouldn't right now. He wasn't taking her seriously. "First, you are only here to observe, not actively participate."

"I doubt that but we will talk about that later," he said. "What else?"

"I'm not a green lawyer," she said, controlling her anger. "I've got more cases under my belt than you realize."

He held up his hand, shaking his head. "Listen, Reagan. I'm not here to validate whether or not you are a good lawyer. I've reviewed your previous cases. You are a great lawyer."

Reagan felt her cheeks go hot as she listened to his words. He had reviewed her previous cases? How much more had he looked up on her? Damn, now she wished she had done more research on him! "I, thanks."

"You're welcome," he answered. "Now, when do we leave?"

Reagan looked away, busying herself by gathering her laptop and notebooks that held all the handwritten notes she had collected throughout her review of the case. His words had made her feel flustered, some of her anger fading away about him being involved on the case. He thought she was a great lawyer. Well, she was about to show him what she could do.

Chapter 3

Greg shifted in his seat, wishing he had taken his wallet out of his back pocket before climbing into the car. He and Reagan were on their way to the Hamptons to interview their client and prep him for trial and had been on the road for about an hour. The weather was great, the sun bright without a cloud in the sky and had he been back home in Texas, he would have been riding around in his convertible with the top down, enjoying the day. But instead he was sitting in the passenger side of a four-door vehicle, with the tension inside thick enough to cut with a knife. Reagan had not said one word since they had left the office and climbed in the car, but he knew she was unhappy that he was coming along for the ride.

"So," he started, knowing it was going to be a long car ride if he didn't at least try to strike up a conversation with her. "Care to fill me in on this case from your perspective?"

She pushed up her sunglasses on her nose. "You've seen the case notes."

"Yes I have," he responded, lifting one shoulder up in a shrug. "But I want to hear what you think."

She sighed loudly and Greg wondered if she was going to say anything else. How were they going to even work together if they couldn't communicate?

"The victim was Greta Tilman," she finally started, her eyes on the road. "A twenty-three-year-old student who was bartending to pay her way through college. She was just an average person, with no ties to anyone that can be directly related to the senator's family or close circle of friends."

"No ties?" Greg asked, though he knew she was right. He too had done some research on the victim, finding nothing exciting about her background or her circle of friends. She had been from Nebraska, trying to make it in the big city, like a great deal of people who flocked to New York each year.

"Not a one," Reagan answered, her voice losing some of the edge from earlier. "I don't even think they knew each other very well. Her co-workers told me that Ben had been a frequent patron of the bar that she worked at but they never saw them do anything together beyond casual conversation."

"Do you think they had a secret relationship?" Greg asked. Something wasn't really adding up in the sense that Ben Kilner, a senator's son with nothing but a few misdemeanors on his record for public drunkenness, would kill a woman he did not even know.

"I don't know," Reagan said, blowing out a breath as she turned the car to the right, following the road to their destination. "Once the detectives couldn't find a link, they quit searching. I put out some feelers with some of my contacts to investigate, but they didn't find anything either."

"Do you think he did it?" Greg asked cautiously, needing to know how much of an uphill battle they were going to have with the defense.

"No," she said softly. "I don't think he did it."

Greg nodded and looked out the window. At least they had that going for them. It was always hard to defend someone you knew was guilty, but it was a hazard of the job. Not everyone was innocent.

They rode in silence a little longer before Reagan pulled into a driveway with large iron gates blocking the view of the house beyond. After she pressed the button on the speaker just outside the gate, they waited.

"Can I help you?" a disembodied voice said crisply a moment later.

"I'm Reagan Lister, Mr. Kilner's counsel."

"Of course, Ms. Lister, please drive forward."

The gates swung inward and Reagan maneuvered the car up the steep drive to pull in front of the large home, giving Greg his first glimpse of the senator's vacation home. It was a mansion, though nothing else would have been expected considering this was an expensive row of houses along the sandy shores of the Hamptons, known for their celebrity summer parties. A man stood on the front step as they exited the car and Greg recognized him as Senator Kilner, a large man dressed in a pair of khakis and a golf shirt, his salt-and-pepper hair blowing in the soft breeze.

"Senator Kilner," Reagan said as she approached the senator, a warm smile on her face. "I apologize that we have come sooner than expected."

"No, it's alright," the senator responded, looking over at Greg. "Who are you?"

Greg stuck out his hand, a warm smile on his face as well. "Greg Pilster. I'm helping out on your son's trial."

"Did you say Pilster?" the senator asked, his eyes widening slightly. "You're the guy from Houston, the lawyer, right?"

"Yes sir," Greg answered as he shook the senator's hand. "It's a pleasure, sir."

"Likewise," the senator murmured, releasing his hand. "Glad to see that Fitz is pulling out all the stops to get my boy out of this hellacious mess. Come on in."

Greg looked over at Reagan and winced as he saw the displeasure on her face. Well hell. All the niceties in the car had just gone out of the window with the senator's words. He motioned for her to go inside first and she flipped her hair over her shoulder before following the senator inside. Greg chuckled to himself as he followed her. He had to give it to her, Reagan Lister was not one to let him off lightly.

The interior of the house was just as spectacular as the exterior, the sunken living room positioned in front of a wall of glass that gave a sweeping view of the beach and the ocean beyond. "Have a seat," the senator said, gesturing toward the furniture scattered about the room. A woman dressed in a maid's uniform came forth immediately and set a tray of lemonade on the coffee table, then disappeared into the house without a word. Reagan took the chair closest to the senator, who settled himself in a wingback chair. Greg chose the couch opposite the two. "I'm glad you are here," the senator continued once everyone was settled. "Ben is nervous about the trial."

"Well you know I, er, we will help him through the trial," Reagan replied, cutting him a sidelong glance. "I'm more concerned about his interview. I don't advise it for my client."

The senator's eyebrows knitted together in anger. "Why? I'm the one who set it up. It's a good way for him to prove his innocence."

"I understand your rationale," Reagan continued, unwavering under the senator's direct gaze. "But a client should never go on TV without being prepped. There isn't enough time."

The senator gave her a look before turning his gaze to Greg. "What do you think? Should he go through with this interview?"

Greg didn't dare look at Reagan. He bet she was hot under the collar about being dismissed by the senator. "I have to side with Ms. Lister on this one," he said slowly, being careful with his words. "In this case, your son needs to focus on the trial. We will help him prove his innocence."

The senator looked as if he was about to blow a gasket, his face becoming mottled with anger. "So, you want me to call the news station back and say never mind? Do you not understand how that will look for me and my boy?"

Greg shifted in his chair, forcing himself to remain calm. "While I don't think it's a good idea, we don't have much of a choice in following through with this interview. Don't worry, Ms. Lister and I will prep your son thoroughly. He will look like a star."

The senator's face lost some of its anger as he pushed out of the chair. "See that he does. I will accept nothing else. Ben is in the guest cottage. I'll have someone show you there."

Chapter 4

Reagan fell in step beside Greg as they followed the woman from before down the crushed shell path to the cottage that was a smaller replica of the main house, the wind coming off the ocean catching her hair and blowing it around her head. She was still surprised at the conversation that had just happened in the main house, the way that Greg had sided with her about the idea of Ben doing a TV interview. But then he hadn't stuck to his guns and folded under the senator's rage. That pissed her off more than anything. Ben going on TV was a very bad idea and she was going to try to talk Ben into not doing it, regardless of the wrath of the senator after the fact.

The maid opened the door and they walked inside. Ben was sitting on the couch when they walked in. He stood and wiped his hands on his cuffed jeans nervously as they approached. "Reagan, I mean Ms. Lister."

"Ben," she answered, clasping her hands in front of her. Ben Kilner was a handsome young man barely in the throes of adulthood, with blond hair that fell over his forehead repeatedly, his blue eyes still showing a hint of fear in them. She knew he was scared to death about going to prison for life. After his arraignment and subsequent bail, he had told her just that. Ben's mother had lost custody of her young son to the senator in a bitter divorce. Ben seldom saw her and Reagan knew he had no other motherly figure in his life. She doubted it was easy living with a man like the senator. "How are you?"

"I-I'm good," he said, looking at Greg with a critical eye. Reagan sighed and turned toward Greg, who was sizing up the man they had to prove innocent. "This is Greg Pilster. He's going to be working on your trial case with me." She was resigned to the fact that she couldn't get rid of him, but it damn well didn't mean she had to like the idea of him sniffing around her case.

Greg nodded toward Ben and there was some awkward silence before Ben looked around nervously. "So, I guess you know that I'm doing that interview tomorrow."

"I don't think it's a good idea," Reagan said immediately. "We need to prep you for trial, Ben."

"Yeah, I know," Ben answered, crossing his arms over his chest. "But dad said it will help with my trial. He said I needed to garner sympathy if I wanted to beat this. I-I can't back out. It will make me look bad."

"Of course not," Greg piped in before Reagan could respond. She wanted to slap the easygoing smile off his face. "But this is it, Ben. After this one, we do nothing else until we put you on the stand, okay?"

"Yeah, sure," Ben replied, shooting a glance at Reagan. She gave him a wan smile, irritated and in sore need of a bubble bath and a glass of good wine. This day was continually going downhill.

They all sat down in the living room, Reagan choosing a chair so that she wouldn't have to sit next to Greg. "So, Ben, tell us what has been going on since we last spoke?"

Ben fidgeted with the cuff of his jeans, not meeting her eye. "I've been receiving death threats."

"I'm sorry about that," Reagan responded softly. "You know it's part of what happens with this kind of trial. We talked about that." When Ben had first gotten out on bail, he had called her relentlessly about the phone calls he was receiving, threatening his life. They had talked with the police, of course, but Reagan had explained to her client that unfortunately people had garnered their own opinions of whether he was guilty or not. There wasn't much anyone could do about that aspect of being an accused murderer.

Ben nodded, his eyes still focused on his jeans. "I know. I just wish all of this was over with."

"It will be soon," Greg added, giving Reagan a nod. "Is there anything we need to know before we practice for the interview?"

Ben looked up at both of them, his gaze tired. "I didn't do it. I didn't know that girl and I don't know how she got in that penthouse. You gotta help me get out of this. I can't go to prison."

Reagan felt a sudden rush of tears at the worry in Ben's voice, knowing her client was scared to death about going to jail. She had to win this case. She had to help set an innocent man free.

***

Two hours later, Reagan walked out of the cottage, mentally drained. She had to admit, Greg knew what he was talking about. Since they had to do the interview, he had grilled Ben on every possible topic, including all the avenues that the reporter could go down. When they were walking out, Ben was heading to the fridge, no doubt to have a few beers.

"That went well," Greg said as he walked beside her on the way to their car. "Ben's tougher than I thought he was."

Reagan opened the driver's side door, looking at him over the top of the car. "I, yes he is."

They climbed in and Reagan started the car, then followed the circular driveway back to the road. "We will need to come back tomorrow before the interview," he stated as they pulled out onto the main road. "I can finish prepping him then."

Reagan gripped the steering wheel tightly as she made her way to the bed and breakfast. She wanted to tell him that he sucked at his job and that she could take care of it from now on, but she couldn't. Damn him. He had done far better than she could have ever done. Ben already was enamored with Greg and Reagan could just feel her client slipping through her fingers. "You mean we can finish prepping him," she said through clenched teeth.

"Of course, he's your client after all," Greg answered, with amusement in his voice. Reagan said nothing as she pulled up in the bed and breakfast parking lot and shut off the engine. "Well, I hope you have a good evening," she said as she climbed out of the car, then grabbed her overnight bag out of the back seat. He followed and together they walked into the charming house where she had stayed before. The bed and breakfast was very popular because unlike most, they also served dinner to the guests.

"Hello and welcome!" the cheery woman behind the counter said as Reagan approached. "Do you have a reservation?"

"I, no," Reagan said with a smile. "But I was hoping you had an extra room for tonight." She hadn't had time to make a reservation.

The woman's smile dimmed as she looked down at the book in front of her. "No, I'm afraid we are all booked up. Busy weekend, you know."

The Handsome Enemy

Reagan felt Greg move next to her and nearly yelped out in surprise as his arm slipped around her waist, hauling her against him. "Well, babe, I'm sorry. I know you wanted to celebrate here."

Before Reagan could say anything, the woman gave Greg a faint smile. "Celebrate?"

"We just got married," Greg said smoothly as Reagan's mouth dropped open. "Kind of spur of the moment. I was going to take her to Jamaica for our honeymoon and all, but all she could talk about was this charming bed and breakfast."

"Oh my, how romantic," the woman said, her expression softening. "Let me, give me a minute."

Reagan waited until she walked off before she disentangled herself from Greg's grasp, ignoring the way her stomach was fluttering in response. "What are you doing?" she hissed, looking at him.

"Getting us a room," he said with a sly smile. "Hey, it was either us being married or you being pregnant. I figured you would want to drink some wine tonight."

"You're insane," she responded, not believing that he was doing this. Them? Married? Absolutely not. He was not her type at all, though Reagan wasn't so sure she had a type anymore.

"I might be," he chuckled, his eyes glittering with laughter. "But I'll bet you twenty bucks this works."

"Done," she countered, crossing her arms over her chest. He winked at her and she looked away, feeling the heat rise to her cheeks once more. It was but a moment later that the woman returned, a flush on her cheeks. "I made some calls and I got you a room if you still want it."

"We do," Greg answered as Reagan growled in defeat. He had done it. He had gotten them a room. Them? She waited until she had paid for the room with her company credit card and they had gotten up the stairs before she rounded on him, putting a hand on his chest. "We are not sharing a room."

He looked at her for a moment before his lips split in a grin. "We are sharing a room, wife. What would they think if you kicked me out on our wedding night?"

Reagan shook her head, feeling the day's events draining her energy as she dropped her hand. "I'm sorry. Thanks for getting the room but I can't, I mean we can't."

Greg laughed then. "Listen, Reagan, I'm not asking you to have sex with me."

"Good," she said quickly, crossing her arms over her chest. "Because I'm not going to have sex with you." She was not even going to consider climbing into bed with the enemy. He was her enemy, right?

"I didn't expect you to," he said. She gave him a hard look and turned, walking quickly to her, no their room and inserting the key. This was crazy. She couldn't share a room with him!

Pushing open the door, Reagan walked in, spying the king-sized bed that dominated the room. The bay window gave her a great view of the ocean a block over and normally she would sigh in happiness and contentment, but knowing that Greg was following her into the room killed her happy mood. She heard the door shut and forced herself to turn around to face him. "Well, what are we going to do then?"

He spied the chaise lounge in the corner and grimaced. "I guess that will be my bed for the night," Greg said, his voice lacking any excitement about having to sleep on the chaise.

Reagan felt a twinge of sympathy for him at the thought of him sleeping on the chaise. He did get them the room after all but there was no way she was going to trade that comfortable, large bed for that uncomfortable-looking chaise that had clearly seen better days. "I, um, yeah, I'm going to take a bath now," she said hastily before escaping to the bathroom, where an old-fashioned tub sat waiting for her. Once she had closed the door to the bathroom, Reagan sagged against it, rubbing a hand over her face. Her day had clearly gone from bad to worse.

Chapter 5

Greg walked down the stairs toward the dining room that was located on the first floor of the bed and breakfast, smoothing his hair back with the palms of his hands on the way. After Reagan had cloistered herself in the bathroom he had disappeared for a while, giving her the space she needed. He had found a quiet reading room where he had checked his emails from his own laptop and made some calls, following up on some of his other business. When he had gotten back to the room, she was gone. Sighing, Greg tried to think about her side of this unlikely partnership between the two of them. He could only imagine what she was thinking, not only being stuck with him on this case, but now forced to share a room for the night. When he had returned, she was gone so he had taken full advantage of the bathroom and now was in search of Reagan. With the car still in the parking lot, there was only one place she could be. Greg walked into the dining room and found it set up for intimate dining, small tables placed about the room and extending out onto the wraparound porch through a set of French doors. Reagan was not in the room itself so he walked out onto the porch and found her seated at the far table that overlooked a fragrant floral garden still blooming in early November. The candlelight framed her face and for a moment he was struck by her beauty as she enjoyed a glass of wine. He knew she would not like his intrusion, but he was going to do it anyway.

"Hey, there you are," he said as he approached the table and took the empty chair. She looked at him and set down her glass, the glare on her face telling him all he needed to know.

"What do you want?" she asked softly.

"A good meal," he answered honestly, his stomach growling in return. "And a cold beer."

A ghost of a smile appeared on her lips before it was gone again and the angry woman was back. "Well, you can go sit anywhere you would like."

Greg sat back, crossing his arms over his chest, enjoying the contest. It had been a long time since a woman had challenged him like this, especially a beautiful one. "I could," he responded. "But then our hostess would wonder if I had already made you upset on our wedding night."

She cleared her throat and looked away. "I wish you wouldn't have told her that."

Before he could respond, their hostess was at the table, a smile on her weathered face. "How are the lovebirds? Is the room to your liking?"

"It's perfect, thank you," Greg said, giving the older woman a smile. He gave her his order and she left them alone again, with a promise to bring something special for the newlyweds.

"I hate deceiving her," Reagan said softly when they were alone. "She really thinks we are married."

"It's only for the night," Greg reminded her gently. "Don't worry about it. Let's talk about the case. What's your suspicion?"

"I really don't know," Reagan sighed, staring at her half-empty glass. "I know he's innocent but he's not going to come across well to the jury. A spoiled rich kid with a daddy in politics, that's what they will see."

Greg couldn't help but agree. That was going to be exactly how not only the jury but also the public judged Ben when the interview was done tomorrow. He had some ideas to make him more sympathetic, but his identity, well, he couldn't do anything about that. "Who are your suspects?" he asked as their hostess brought his beer and refilled Reagan's wineglass before disappearing once more.

She looked up in surprise. "Suspects?"

He chuckled. "Come on. I'm a lawyer too. Don't tell me you haven't compiled a listing of who could be suspects." It was another hazard of the job. Anytime he felt that his client was completely innocent, he turned into a detective, wanting to solve the case on behalf of the victim.

She gave him a small smile. "Okay, so I do have a list but it's a short one."

Greg took a sip of his beer before settling back. "Go ahead, lay it on me."

She hesitated, grabbing her wineglass and taking a sip. Greg waited, hoping that this was a way to loosen her up a little. They needed to work together, but the hostility she had for him even being here despite how much he was attempting to help her out was killing their partnership. "Fine," she finally said. "I've got a list. I think it's an inside job to frame the son and make the father look bad."

"So political motivation," he answered.

She nodded and drained her glass as their food arrived. "Yes. Why else would someone set Ben up?"

Greg couldn't help but agree. The guy had no ties to anything illegal nor did he act like someone who would kill the girl in cold blood. "She was strangled. Do you think the jury will look at it as a crime of passion?"

Reagan shrugged as she pinched off a piece of her fish with her fork. "Maybe. They found no evidence of sexual contact though they did find Ben's DNA on her body. It's a concern of mine."

Greg cut into his steak and popped a piece in his mouth, chewing on it thoughtfully. The DNA did make the case harder to defend and if Ben didn't do it, then how did his DNA get on the victim? Those were the types of questions he knew ran through jurors' and the public's minds.

They finished their meal in relative silence, then took their time to walk back to the room side by side. Reagan opened the door and gasped, causing Greg to rush in, thinking something horrible had happened. "Oh," he said, taking in the sight. Candles were lit everywhere, with rose petals nearly covering the king bed. A bottle of champagne was sitting in the chiller beside the bed, waiting to be opened and enjoyed.

Reagan turned toward him, her eyes flashing anger. "See? I told you, you shouldn't have told her we were married!"

Greg laughed, because he couldn't do anything else as Reagan stomped off, blowing out the candles along the way. When she was done, she pulled back the cover on the bed, sending rose petals flying all over the room before throwing the cover at him, along with a pillow. "Good night," he called as she stalked to the bathroom. The door slammed behind her and Greg walked over to his bed for the night, throwing the cover on the chaise. Well, at least it hadn't been a boring night.

***

The sound of the door opening woke her up out of a dreamless sleep and Reagan at first thought she was at home, in her own bed. Then she realized she was still in the Hamptons, sharing a room with the enemy who was waking her up in the middle of the night. She looked over from her vantage point and felt her heart stop as she saw Greg's form still lying on the chaise not far from the bed, realizing he wasn't the one who had opened the door. He was still asleep. Biting her lip, Reagan strained to hear any sound, catching the faint sound of boots on the wooden floor as they crept closer to the bed. Someone was in the room and she doubted it was their hostess coming to give them another special treatment. Quickly Reagan tried to come up with her options. She could scream, wake Greg up and hope that their intruder did not have a gun. If he did, they both could be dead. She could jump up and surprise the intruder, but again, if he had a gun, they were both dead. So, she did the only thing she could think of and rolled off the bed, the sound of her body hitting the floor a loud thud. Greg jumped up immediately and the sound of boots retreating vibrated through the floor as the intruder fled.

"Reagan?"

Reagan pushed herself off the floor with a grunt, her elbow stinging from the quick decision. "I'm fine."

Greg was at her side a moment later, concern on his face as he helped her to her feet. "Someone was in the room."

He looked over at the open door and was gone in a flash, his bare feet slapping on the wood as he ran down the hall. Reagan grabbed her robe from the end of the bed and threw it around her pajamas, her hands shaking as she smoothed her hair back off her head. Why would someone be in their room? It didn't make any sense.

Greg returned a few moments later, his hair sticking up on his head. Reagan realized then that he was bare-chested, his tanned, muscular frame a great deal bigger now that he wasn't wearing his suit. "Whoever it was is gone," he said. "I found the doors opened in the dining room. I doubt they were locked to begin with."

Reagan wrapped her arms around herself, feeling a sudden chill in the room. "Who do you think it was?"

Greg crossed the room, stopping a few inches in front of her. "Are you okay?"

She forced herself to nod. "I'm fine. I haven't fallen off the bed since I was a kid."

"It was good quick thinking," Greg said, giving her a small smile. "I'm sorry. I sleep like the dead."

Reagan cleared her throat, feeling somewhere between hysterical and calm. Someone had been in the room. Greg must have sensed her panic for he reached out, barely touching her arm with his warm hand. "Hey," he said softly. "It's going to be okay. I'll stay up if you want to go back to sleep."

Touched far too much by his kindness, she shook her head as she looked at the clock on the bedside table. "No, we only have about an hour until sunrise."

He nodded and dropped his hand. "I'm going to find our hostess then. Lock the door behind me."

Reagan watched him leave before crossing the room and throwing the door closed, locking it soundly before sagging against it. This wasn't just a random, hey let's visit a room and scare the bejesus out of them kind of visit. This had to be targeted but why? Why would someone want to harm either of them?

Pushing away from the door, she flipped on the light and gasped as she saw just how close she had come to being in serious danger. A knife was buried in the pillow next to hers, the handle barely visible among the covers. Reagan felt all the blood drain from her face, her knees weakening slightly. This wasn't just some random intruder. This intruder intended to harm her.

Chapter 6

Two hours later she and Greg were back in the car, the bellies full of coffee in an effort to keep them both alert. Their hostess had apologized profusely about the intruder, wanting to fill out a police report but since nothing was taken and no one was harmed, Reagan had waved off the idea. Besides, they had no idea who it was nor had she gotten a look at the person. It would be a futile report. Still, the knife stuck in her mind as they had pulled away from the bed and breakfast, a single indication that someone meant business. Greg had said nothing when he had arrived back in the room, seeing the knife and her pale face, and she was certain he didn't know what to say really. The proof was there.

As she pulled into the senator's drive, Reagan noticed the large amounts of media parked along the road, giving her some worry. She had expected one or two trucks for this interview, not the entire fleet. The gates were closed and as Reagan rolled down the window to press the button, her car was surrounded by media. "Ms. Lister!" one of the reporters called out, shoving a microphone in her face. "Are you prepared to defend your client?"

The Handsome Enemy

"What the hell?" Greg asked next to her as Reagan rang the bell, hoping that the gates would open soon. "Where did they come from?"

"Ms. Lister!" the reporter tried again as Reagan tried to push the microphone out of her face. "All the evidence points to Ben. How do you anticipate his interview to help with the case?"

"No comment," Reagan replied as the gates started to open slowly. Without waiting for the reporter to get her hand out of the car window, she pulled forward, the microphone hitting the side of the car and disappearing out of the window. The gates closed immediately behind them as she pulled the car up to the front door and they climbed out. "Where did they all come from?" Greg asked again, looking back at the cluster of reporters viewable beyond the gate.

"I guess they all want an exclusive interview," Reagan replied as they were admitted into the house by the maid from the day before. The room had been transformed into a mini TV studio, the bright lights focused on the two chairs that would serve as the hot seat for her client today. The interviewer was to be a hardnosed reporter who was known for her tough questions, which was another reason Reagan was extremely glad they had grilled Ben so hard yesterday. Now any questions she threw at him were going to be a walk in the park as long as he stuck to the answers they had practiced.

The Handsome Enemy

"I still think this is a bad idea," she said as they waited for the senator to arrive in the room. "What if he missteps? What if he says something wrong?"

"We will deal with it," Greg answered as the senator and the reporter entered the room.

"Thank you, senator, for your time," she said, shaking his hand. "I'm sorry this didn't work out exactly as we had hoped today."

The senator gave the reporter a warm smile as he walked her to the door. "I appreciate your willingness to keep this under wraps for now. I promise you will have the exclusive story as soon as we are able to set it up." The reporter gave them both a glance as she made her way out of the house, the senator shutting the door behind her before wiping a hand over his face, his expression not at all friendly. Reagan felt the first stirring of worry as he looked at them, wondering what was going on here. "Ms. Lister, Mr. Pilster," the senator said, acknowledging their presence. "We have a problem."

"Problem?" Reagan echoed with a frown. "What kind of problem?"

"It's Ben," the senator answered, annoyance in his voice. "He's gone."

Reagan's blood seized in her body as she heard the senator's words. Ben was gone? Where? Why? He seemed fine yesterday, maybe a little nervous but fine. "When did you find this out?" she asked.

"This morning," the senator replied, clearly not concerned about his son. That gave Reagan pause. If her child was missing, she would be frantic with worry. "That little snot is going to make himself look like a guilty man if he doesn't get back here."

Reagan ignored the blatant comment from the senator and placed her hands on her hips. "Where did he go?"

"Hell, I don't know," the senator said darkly. "But you have to find him."

"We aren't the police," Greg said. Reagan had forgotten he was beside her. "By the way, where are the police?"

"Are you kidding me?" the senator asked, arching a brow. "If I call the cops, he's going to jail and it will look like there is no question about his guilt. No, we aren't calling the cops. I'm not losing my bond money because my son got cold feet about this interview. You are going to find him and bring him back here."

"I, we can't do that," Reagan added, shooting a glance at Greg. That wasn't their job. She had a bigger issue now that she had a client as a runner, but to find him? Surely the senator had some detectives in his back pocket he could call or something.

"You will do it," the senator announced, pointing at her. "Or I will ruin your career. Both of you. You were the last ones to talk to my son. You were the ones who caused this."

"You were the one who scheduled the interview," Greg shot back, anger in his voice. "If anyone, you caused him to run."

The senator's face turned red and Reagan knew Greg had just pissed him off. "Watch yourself, son. I don't care who you are, I can destroy you with a few calls."

"Come on, Greg," Reagan urged, turning to go. They didn't have a choice. They were going to have to find Ben and bring him back. The senator wasn't going to accept anything else and she could not afford for her entire career to be upended.

Together they walked out to the car and climbed in, Reagan sitting behind the steering wheel, her mind running in a hundred different places. If she were wanted by the police, where would she go?

"I can't believe the gall of that man," Greg said, disgust in his voice. "His son is missing and all he can care about is the bond money? What kind of father is he?"

"We should call the police," she answered, though her voice lacked determination. "It would be the right thing to do."

"It would be," Greg said slowly. "But it wouldn't help your case whatsoever."

Reagan looked over at him, the day's events giving her a headache. "I know. I'm torn."

Greg gave her a look and then sighed, rubbing a hand over his face. "So, we are now detectives or better yet, bond chasers."

"I can't lose my job," she said gently, hating that she was in this predicament. She was a lawyer not a people finder! This was crazy. They needed to call Martin, let him in on this drastic turn of events.

"Yeah, me neither," Greg said, leaning back in the seat. "Well, where do you think he went?"

Reagan shook her head, trying to think of where her client would disappear to. He couldn't fly out of the country because his passport had been confiscated upon his release on bail. So, that meant he was in a car. "I think he's heading back to New York." After all, there was nowhere else he could go on the island.

"New York," Greg echoed. "We will never find him."

A thought came to Reagan and she started the engine, her mouth set in a determined line. She knew where he was heading. Why, was the other question.

***

Greg watched Reagan out of the corner of his eye, wondering what was going through that pretty head of hers. She hadn't said a word since they had pulled away from the senator's home, a place that Greg hoped to not visit again anytime soon. What had seemed like just a case he was going to help a green lawyer get through had taken an interesting turn and Greg could feel the adrenaline pumping through his blood at the thought of what they were going to encounter. Reagan had called Martin on their way back to the city, telling him everything that had happened. The answer she got from her boss was to do everything they could to keep the cops from finding out that Ben was missing and to keep the senator happy. So, the green light was given and now they were about to rush headlong into potential danger. It was not the exact turn of events he had thought would happen, but exciting nevertheless.

Shifting in the seat, Greg cleared his throat. "So do you want to let me in on your grand plan? I can see it written all over your face."

"I think I know where he's going," she finally answered as they passed the sign stating they had less than an hour before they arrived in Manhattan. "Why he's going there, I don't know."

"Why would he run?" Greg asked aloud, the question hanging heavily over his head. It didn't make any sense. If the guy was as innocent as Reagan believed him to be, then there would be no real reason to worry. Well, other than the mountain they were going to have to climb to make him look innocent to the jury. That he hadn't been worried about until today. Now he wasn't so sure he could win this case.

"Scared?" Reagan offered with a shrug. "Intimidated by the interview? This is a lot for someone to handle."

Greg nodded absently. Both were plausible reasons, but none of them made sense, not to him at least. "What's your thought on the senator?"

Reagan blew out a breath as the city appeared in the distance. "I don't like the guy. He thrives on intimidation and I think he is able to manipulate his son into doing whatever he believes is the right thing. I think he's part of the reason Ben left."

Greg didn't answer, instead trying to sort out all the facts in his head about the case and the recent turn of events. He'd never had a client just up and disappear, most were too scared of the cops or breaking their bail to do so. Something had spooked Ben, something big.

Reagan maneuvered the car to a tall high-rise near the center of Manhattan, one that Greg recognized as the scene of the murder. "You think he went back here?" he asked as Reagan found a parking spot in front of the building and cut the engine.

"I'm not sure," she admitted, opening the door. "But it's a good guess at least."

Greg climbed out of the car and together they walked into the building. The building housed luxury apartments and penthouses, largely owned by celebrities. He had looked into the building when he first received the case file, finding that it offered all the amenities of privacy. The senator's penthouse was located on the top floor, offering panoramic views of Manhattan, and had been purchased at a lofty sum. Ben had been living there for the last year, up until the murder. "How are we going to gain access?" he asked Reagan as they approached the key card access only elevator. Reagan pursed her lips, looking around the surprisingly simple lobby. "Good question. This is when I wish I was more like a detective instead of a lawyer."

Greg grinned as he spied a woman approaching the elevator, attempting to control her two small yapping dogs. "Come on," he said, hurrying over. The woman was elderly. There was the unmistakable flash of diamonds on her gnarled hands as she attempted to find her pass card in her purse. "Excuse me, ma'am," Greg said, a warm smile on his face. "Can I be of assistance?"

The Handsome Enemy

She looked up, a grateful smile on her face. "You sure can, young man. Will you hold Butch and Cassidy while I find my card?"

Greg took over the leashes of the small dogs, giving Reagan a wink as she stood nearby. The woman found her card and pressed it against the small black box, the elevator doors immediately sliding open. Greg followed her into the elevator, Reagan sliding in just as the doors were about to close. "Thank you," the woman said as Greg handed the leashes back.

"Not a problem," he answered as Reagan pushed the button for the top floor. They rode for a few seconds before the woman's floor arrived and she got off the elevator, leaving the two of them alone as the doors slid closed.

"That was smart thinking," Reagan said softly as the elevator resumed its ascent. "I would have never thought to do something like that. Are you sure you are a lawyer?"

Greg grinned, crossing his arms over his chest. "Well I might have had a small stint as a private investigator to pay my way through college. You pick up all kinds of tricks from that trade. I saw a woman needing a rescue. A smile, a kind word, and most people will not think twice."

"I would," she frowned. "People shouldn't be so trusting."

The doors opened and Greg walked out first into the small foyer that led to the front door of the penthouse. "Maybe you should be more trusting, Reagan." It was clear to him that she was not his biggest fan, their unlikely partnership already off to a rocky start. He skidded to a stop as he noted that the main penthouse doors were slightly ajar. He held his hand out to stop Reagan as she came up beside him. There were no sounds coming from beyond the doors, the space eerily quiet.

"Someone is here," Reagan whispered as Greg inched his way to the door. "We should call the police."

"Not yet," Greg said softly, nudging the door open wider with his foot. Just inside he could see that the place had been ransacked, a few chairs turned over on the marble floor in the living room, papers strewn all over the place. Reagan took a step forward and he shot out an arm, holding her back. "No, don't," he said softly. "Someone might still be here."

"But Ben might be in there," she said urgently, worry in her voice. "We can't just leave."

Greg drew in a breath. "I'll go check."

Reagan looked at him, clear surprise on her face. He gave her a grin and walked inside the penthouse before he could change his mind. It wasn't the first idiotic thing he had done for a woman in his life, he just hoped it wasn't the last.

Chapter 7

Reagan paced the small entryway to the penthouse, expecting at any moment to hear gunshots. A tossed apartment was an indication that someone was looking for something or someone, though she wasn't quite sure what that could be. And Greg. The man was crazy. A small piece of her was surprised that he would risk his life to go in search of her, no their, client like this and every passing moment, she worried about him. He was definitely not turning out to be the uptight lawyer she had anticipated and the thought scared her that she could actually be attracted to him. She didn't want to, but her traitorous body was starting rapidly to really like Greg.

A sound caught her attention and she turned to see Greg walking out, looking no worse for wear. Relief flooded Reagan's body as she walked over to him. "There's no one in there," he said, rubbing a hand over his face. "Someone has wrecked the place good but I didn't see any signs of Ben or anyone else."

"Great, that was my only lead," Reagan sighed. Where was her client and what had spooked him into running? She had to find him before word got out. A suspected murderer on the run would not play very well with the jury if they made it to trial.

"No friends, no one else?" Greg asked as they turned and walked back to the elevator. "What about Ben's mother?"

Reagan shook her head. "The senator and his wife have been divorced for twenty years. His mother is currently living in Paris." There would be no way Ben would get through security without a passport anyway.

Greg jabbed at the button, the doors sliding open so that they could both step inside. Reagan tried to think of other people that Ben associated with, anything that might help her locate him. She was truly worried about her client. The elevator ride was short and soon they were climbing back in her car. "I guess we need to head back to the office and fill in Martin," she said as she pulled out into traffic. "Maybe he can think of something I haven't."

Greg didn't say anything, looking in the side mirror with a frown on his face. "I think we are being followed."

"What?" Reagan asked, looking into her rearview mirror. All she saw was the jumbled mass of cars that were common in Manhattan, a flurry of taxicabs and dark sedans.

"There's an SUV two cars back," Greg answered, looking in the mirror. "They pulled out the same time we did."

The Handsome Enemy

Reagan swallowed hard, her palms sweaty from her grip on the steering wheel. What had her life become over the last forty-eight hours? She was a lawyer, for god's sake, but felt like the target in some kind of weird action movie. "What do we do?" she asked, her eyes on the road before her.

"Get on the interstate," Greg said, pointing to the exit in the distance. "Let's see if we can lose them."

"This is crazy," Reagan said, turning onto the exit ramp. They got onto the multi-lane road and she tried to not seem nervous, when on the inside she was falling apart.

Greg constantly looked in all the mirrors, not saying anything as she flowed with the traffic. "Take the next exit," he said abruptly. Reagan peeled off the road down the exit, narrowly missing the concrete barrier in the process. Her pulse was pounding, her adrenaline pumping but all she wanted to do was get home and crawl under the covers.

The hit from behind came out of nowhere. "Shit," Greg said, his hands grabbing the dashboard. "Drive! Drive!"

Reagan pressed on the gas, looking frantically in the rearview mirror as the SUV suddenly loomed behind the car. The next hit wasn't so much of a surprise and Reagan winced as she heard the crumple of her bumper. "Hang on," she said, a tremor in her voice as

The Handsome Enemy

she turned sharply to the right, pulling out into traffic headed back to the city. Heedless of the speed limit, she dodged cars left and right, Greg helping her duck in and out of lanes.

"Turn there, now!" Greg shouted, pointing to a cluster of buildings on her right. Reagan cut across four lanes of traffic and got onto the exit in the nick of time, pulling in between the buildings until she couldn't go any farther due to the narrowing of the buildings toward the end of the alleyway. Greg turned around, watching as they sat there, waiting for the next thing that would happen.

"I think you lost them," he finally said, turning to look at her. Reagan couldn't speak, her heart in her throat. She had just been in a high-speed chase through the streets of Manhattan. Suddenly she couldn't deal with it anymore. She threw open the door and stepped out, ignoring the fact that they were in an alley loaded with trash dumpsters. This was not her life. This was not what should be happening to her! Why were they targeting her now? Why was this happening?

"Hey it's okay," Greg said from behind her, his hands on her shaking shoulders. "It's going to be okay."

Reagan whirled around to face him, hating the fact that he was seeing her in such a mess. "How do you know?" she asked, emotion in her voice. "We were just chased. Someone murdered my pillow at the bed and breakfast. It's not looking good for me at all."

Greg's jaw clenched tightly as he looked at her, his hands warm on her shoulders. "It's going to be fine, Reagan," he said firmly. "I'm not going to let anything happen to you." Before she knew it, he was pulling her against him, his arms surrounding her. Reagan felt her breath leave her lungs as she took in Greg's clean, crisp scent, the way his hard body was pressed up against hers. His hands were splayed on her back, comforting and not at all in any other manner. She felt her body sag against him, reveling in his warmth, and wrapped her arms around his neck, against her better judgment. She just wanted to be comforted, to be held.

"You are going to be fine," he murmured against her ear, his hands stroking her back lightly. "I swear it, Reagan."

Reagan shuddered, not from her fear anymore, but the way she was feeling in Greg's arms. When was the last time she had allowed a man to simply hold her? Quite a while and he was nowhere as handsome as Greg was. Or brave. She wasn't seeing him as the enemy anymore and the thought scared her. Flustered, she pulled out of his arms, putting some distance between them. "I'm sorry," she said, her voice shaking. "I don't know what came over me."

The Handsome Enemy

"Hey it's fine," Greg said, shoving his hands in his pockets. "It's a stressful time. I think someone is out to get you, Reagan, or us both. Who knows, at this point."

"That's ridiculous," she answered with a shake of her head. "I haven't done anything except my job."

Greg kicked at an empty bottle with his shoe. "First the bed and breakfast incident and now this. I believe your life is in danger."

Reagan felt the blood drain from her face. Her life in danger? She knew that there was always a potential given her chosen profession. After all, she was dealing with clients who may or may not end up in jail. Taking a high-profile case like this, it doubled her risk but not until now had she actually had any issues. "That's crazy," she said softly.

"I don't think you should be alone," Greg said, holding out his hand. "Give me the keys. We will go to my place."

Reagan let out a little laugh as she looked at him. "Your place?"

"Yes," he said. "If you are in danger, someone is probably watching your place as we speak. It's not safe for you to go back. I doubt they even know where I'm staying so mine will be safe for the moment."

"I'll call the cops," she answered. "They will send a detail. I will be fine."

Greg started to walk toward her, his face showing anger. "Come on, don't be difficult, Reagan. What are you going to tell them anyway? You've lost your client?"

Reagan opened her mouth to retort, realizing that he was right. What would she tell the police anyway? Anything she said that was remotely true would put not only her entire case on the rocks but also put Ben in trouble. She couldn't have that. She needed to find him first. "I'll go to a hotel," she finally said. The thought of going to Greg's place had her feeling uncomfortable and not because she didn't want to go. It was because she wanted to go to his place. That had her all out of sorts.

"Don't be ridiculous," he said, beckoning her with his hand. "Give me your keys, Reagan, or I'll call Martin and get him to take you off the case."

"You wouldn't dare," she challenged. "He wouldn't."

Greg blew out a breath, looking frustrated. "He already doesn't think you can handle this case, Reagan. One call about this and you will be looking at a sudden vacation."

"I hate you," she seethed, not believing he would do this. What did he mean Martin didn't think she could handle this case? Was that why he really was here?

"Trust me," Greg tried again. "Please, Reagan. I don't want to see you get hurt."

Reagan wanted to scream in frustration. She hated the fact that Greg was right. She hated the fact that her boss didn't think she could do her job. She hated the fact that Greg was even here, pretending to be her friend but making threats in the same breath. The look on his face told her he wasn't going to let this drop and they could not stand in this awful-smelling alley all day arguing. She had a client to find and though she didn't want to admit it, she needed Greg's help. "Fine," she forced out, throwing the keys at his chest. "But I don't like this."

He chuckled, catching the keys. "I don't expect you to, but you know it's the best option."

Reagan stalked over to the passenger side and climbed in, crossing her arms over her chest. He was right. She had no other options.

***

They arrived at Greg's apartment as the sun was starting to sink into the horizon. Reagan pulled her bag out from their trip to the Hamptons, grateful that she at least had her toiletries. She was not planning on staying any longer than tonight, and once they found Ben, she was going to get Martin to kick Greg to the curb, send him back to Texas. She could handle this case once she got her client under control.

The Handsome Enemy

Looking at her bumper, she winced as she walked past, thinking of the car insurance. It was going to be ugly in terms of money that was going to be shelled out by the firm when she made that claim. Reagan followed Greg into the elevator and rode up in silence, realizing that the apartment building was nicer than her own. Leave it to Martin to pull out all the stops to get Greg to stay. She should demand a raise after all of this. "It's not much," he said as they exited the elevator and walked down the carpeted hall to one of the doors. Greg inserted a key and pushed the door open. "But the fridge is fully stocked."

Reagan clutched her bag as she walked inside, taking in the minimalistic décor and furniture of the living room. The kitchen was sleek as well, the black granite countertops a sharp contrast to the stainless-steel appliances. It was impressive, but she wasn't going to let him know that. "You can have the bedroom," he was saying as he shut the door and locked it soundly. "I'll order some pizza or whatever you like."

"Pizza's fine," she sniffed. "Where's the bedroom?"

He pointed it out and Reagan walked down the hall to the room, shutting the door firmly behind her before letting out a ragged sigh. Her nerves were a hot mess and now she was surrounded by the clean scent of Greg's cologne on the sheets, sleeping in the bed that he had been occupying. Great, just great.

The Handsome Enemy

Throwing her bag onto the bed, Reagan walked over to the window and stared out over the buildings of the city. At least she was safe. Despite what she felt or didn't feel about Greg, she knew that he was being truthful when he said he would protect her. Until she found Ben, Reagan needed his help.

She kicked off her shoes and looked down at her wrinkled business suit, the one she had donned this morning to show the senator and Ben that she was the real deal, a good lawyer that could get his son out of this mess. But now, her day had been turned upside down. With a sigh, she removed the skirt and jacket, then unbuttoned the silk blouse before rummaging in her bag for some comfortable clothes.

The door opened and Greg filled the doorway, his eyes widening as he saw her state of undress. "What are you doing?" Reagan asked, flustered as she grabbed her jacket and held it in front of her.

A dull flush crept over Greg's face as he backed out of the room. "Sorry, I totally forgot you were in here."

"Just get out," she said. He nodded and exited the room, closing the door behind him. Reagan stood there for a moment, goosebumps breaking out over her body. She should be furious, embarrassed, but she hadn't missed the heated look that had flared in his eyes. When was the last time she had been wanted by a man? She had to get this mess over and done with because her thoughts about her "partner" were turning into thoughts she didn't know how to control. Taking a deep breath, she got dressed, making sure to cover every inch of her body though something told her that Greg probably would give her the same look even with clothes on. Ugh, when did this become complicated? She wasn't even supposed to like the guy! With a sigh, she walked out of the bedroom and down the hall as Greg was putting the pizzas on the counter. "Hey, right on time," he said, giving her no indication that he cared to talk about what had happened. That was fine with Reagan. She didn't care to talk about it either.

After rounding up some plates, Greg put them on the counter and Reagan helped herself to the warm pizza, realizing she was ravenous. When had been the last time they had eaten? Her days were starting to run together and Reagan knew it was going to take her quite a while to sort her life back out once she found Ben and got him back to the Hamptons. There was still a case to concentrate on and win, a client to prove innocent though she was finding it harder and harder to believe that her client was still right in maintaining his innocence. Why had Ben run in the first place? Didn't guilty people run and not innocent people?

"So," Greg said as he placed a few beer bottles on the counter, popping the tops and taking a long sip out of one of them. "Why did you become a lawyer?"

"What?" she asked. She had polished off one of the pieces of pizza and was reaching for another.

"Give me a break here," he said, reaching for a slice himself. "I'm trying to make small talk."

Reagan thought about the question, seeing no harm in giving him an answer. "I wanted to do something to help others."

"So you chose law school?" Greg chuckled. "Healthcare would have been a safer bet."

"I used to love watching the court cases on TV," she answered, thinking back to when she used to sit there and try to deduce the evidence and practice her closing remarks. "There's a certain power trip when you are attempting to prove or disprove a case. I figured I would give it a shot."

"I can understand about the power trip," he answered as she grabbed one of the beers. "Like there's an element of surprise forever waiting in the wings."

Reagan nodded, leaning against the counter, full for now. It was nice that someone else could understand her rationale for becoming a lawyer. The challenge had kept her engaged as well and all through law school she had strived to be top of her class just to prove to the naysayers she could do this. Now she was in a world of mess and had a slippery slope to climb up. "What about you?" she asked, trying to steer her thoughts away from her mess for now. "Why did you become a lawyer?"

"I don't know," Greg shrugged, draining his bottle and setting it on the counter. "At one time, I wanted to save the world and since there was no superhero school, the closest thing for sending bad guys to jail was law school. My stint in the private investigator side of things showed me how important it was to be a good lawyer and have good witnesses."

"And good clients," Reagan added, wishing hers hadn't just up and disappeared like that. He could be facing time in prison for just running if anyone caught up with him. They had to find him and fast. Setting down her beer, Reagan clasped her hands in front of her. "Well I'm beat," she said lightly. "I'm going to get some sleep."

He didn't say anything at first, his eyes roaming over her and causing her to shiver inwardly. She had been right. He could undress her with his eyes. "Okay. Don't worry, I won't bother you tonight."

"I, thanks," she said hastily before retreating to the bedroom, shutting the door firmly behind her. This was crazy, this attraction between them in a moment of crisis. Whereas she should be focusing on finding her client, she was chatting it up with the handsome lawyer like they were good friends. Or something more. "No," she said softly to herself, pushing away from the bedroom door she had been leaning against.

There was nothing else here, nothing at all. But as she crawled into Greg's bed, his scent all around her, Reagan knew she was lying to herself.

Chapter 8

Greg was up and dressed the next morning, coffee brewing in the kitchen when Reagan came out of his bedroom, looking like he felt. His night on the couch had been hell. He had been unable to concentrate on sleep when he couldn't get the image of Reagan nearly naked out of his mind. She was gorgeous and he hadn't lied to her when he told her that he had forgotten she was in there. He had, honestly and was glad that he had forgotten.

"Good morning," he said, handing her a mug as she entered the kitchen.

"Morning," she answered, accepting the cup. "Thanks. Coffee is exactly what I need."

"I think there is some breakfast stuff around here if you want something," he said. "Or leftover pizza."

She shook her head, taking a sip of her coffee. "I'm good. Thanks."

Greg nodded, picking up his own mug as well. After his accidental view of her last night, their pizza dinner had been short and painfully awkward before she escaped back into the bedroom for the rest of the night. He hadn't even had a chance to apologize or explain himself. The funny thing was, Greg didn't know if he wanted to apologize. "So what's on the docket today?" he asked, leaning against the counter.

Reagan looked at him, a small smile on her lips. "A little court humor?" she asked.

He grinned. "Maybe."

She placed her mug on the counter, looking down into the murky liquid. "I think we need to update Martin."

Greg nodded, thinking that they needed to keep him in the loop at least. After all, he was the one who was going to sign their paychecks. "Yeah, I agree. He might have thought of something we haven't."

She reached into her pocket and pulled out her cell, the phone ringing nearly immediately. "It's an unknown number," Reagan said, looking up at him. "What if it's Ben?"

"Put it on speaker," Greg said, excitement drumming through him. If it was Ben, they were about to have a major break. Reagan swiped the phone to answer it, putting it on speaker. "Hello?"

"Ms. Lister," a familiar voice filled the room.

"Ben," Reagan said, looking up at Greg. "I am so glad to hear from you."

"I'm sorry," Ben said, emotion evident in his voice. "I-I had no choice. Someone tried to kill me at the cottage. I had to leave."

Reagan looked up at Greg, her eyes widening. Greg held in the swear he wanted to release, not wanting to spook the client. So that's why he left. He couldn't blame him.

"Ben, let me help you," Reagan forced out. "Tell me where you are at and I will come get you."

"I need to leave," Ben said urgently. Greg shook his head, trying to motion to Reagan to keep him talking while he picked up his own phone, shooting a text to a long-ago associate of his. "What's your number?" he mouthed. Reagan signaled her phone number and he shot that text as well, glad that he had kept his associates close.

"Ben, you can't leave," Reagan said as Greg motioned for her to continue to talk. "They will arrest you. I'm sorry to say it but I am your only source of help. Let me help you."

"You can't help me," Ben answered, his voice breaking. "No one can help me."

Greg received the text he was waiting on and gave Reagan a thumbs-up, flipping his phone around so she could see that he knew exactly where Ben was. "Please, Ben," she tried once more, the sound of a dial tone following a moment later.

"We got it," Greg announced, grabbing her keys and his phone. "Come on, let's go get him."

"He sounds so scared," Reagan said as they walked out of the apartment and to the elevator. Greg stabbed the button with his finger. "What could have happened to have him so spooked?"

"I don't know," Greg admitted, a sinking feeling in his gut. Whatever it was, it couldn't be good.

They reached the first floor and hurried to her car. Greg climbed in the driver's seat without even asking. Reagan didn't put up a fight as she piled into the passenger seat and he input the address into the car's GPS system before peeling out of the garage.

"How did you get that address?" she asked, curious.

Greg chuckled, his eyes on the traffic. "Another associate from my previous occupation. He's very good at tracking signals from cell phones though I'm afraid he has your phone number now."

She laughed. "Should I be worried?"

Greg shook his head, turning onto the road that the GPS pointed them toward. "Nah, John is harmless. Just don't be surprised if you get invited to every party he has from now on. He usually invites everyone in his contact list." John was in his forties and enjoyed a good party at his ranch in Texas a few times a year. Greg had been to many, partly because he was scared that John would track him down at his house for not attending, but always enjoyed going. Though John was a bit eccentric, Greg enjoyed his presence in doses. Otherwise, he spent most of his time attempting to decipher what John was saying, especially when John started talking in technical jargon that Greg did not understand.

"That doesn't sound too bad," she answered, a frown on her face. "I can't believe he found him so quickly. I've got a bad feeling about this, Greg, a really bad feeling."

Greg reached over and touched her hand, internally grinning when she didn't pull it away immediately. "We will handle it, okay?"

She nodded, finally withdrawing her hand and tucking it between her legs. Greg kept his eyes on the road, his own worries churning in his gut. What he was afraid of was that Ben had a damn good reason for running and it had nothing to do with the case.

It took them about twenty minutes to get to the location, a run-down motel that advertised clean beds and a swimming pool that looked like it had seen better days. Greg parked the car in the parking lot. "We've got to figure out what room he's in," he said, his fingers drumming along the steering wheel. "I'm afraid John's expertise only allows for so much. There has to be over fifty doors in this joint."

"Not a problem," Reagan replied. Greg watched as she shed her suit jacket, unbuttoning her shirt to reveal the nice swell of her breasts above her lacy camisole. His body went into overdrive, his pants becoming uncomfortably tight in a certain area. Dear god, what had he done to deserve such torture?

"What are you doing?" he finally croaked out, unable to take his eyes off her. She was beautiful. Reagan fluffed her hair with her fingers and gave him a dazzling smile before opening the passenger door. "There's a man tending the counter. I'm going to get that information from him."

She climbed out before he could say anything else, making sure to pull up her skirt to mid-thigh before walking away, leaving him in a daze. God, she was gorgeous and any man would give her whatever she wanted. Greg knew he would. When had she captivated him so much? He couldn't remember, but part of him was dying to have her. If they survived this mess they had gotten themselves into, he was going to work on breaking her down, showing her that he could be good for her. That they could be good for each other.

Reagan was gone only a few moments. A catlike smile was on her face as she approached the car, buttoning her shirt back up. "He's in number fifteen," she said as she straightened her skirt and grabbed her jacket. "That was way too easy."

Greg didn't respond as he climbed out of the car, adjusting his pants along the way. Yeah, it would have been too easy for him to give her what she wanted too if Reagan was coming his way looking like that. "You would have made a good private investigator," he told her. She grinned and adjusted her clothing back to her normal look, though he was pleased to see that she left one of her buttons undone on her shirt.

"Thanks," she said. "If this lawyer thing doesn't pan out, I will look into it. Now let's go." Greg chuckled and followed her up the stairs. She was full of surprises and he was dying to find out every single one of them.

As they approached the door, he grabbed her arm, forcing her behind him. "Let me go first," he said softly as she started to protest. "Just in case."

She put her hand on his arm, holding onto it as they walked up to the door and Greg knocked firmly, fully expecting to hear the rapid fire of a gun as a result. If he had to die at this moment, Reagan clinging to his arm was a good way to end his life. The door opened and Ben's eyes widened as he saw them. He attempted to shut the door but Greg placed his foot in the doorway and forced it back open. They moved inside and he shut the door behind them. "Hey Ben," he said. "Fancy meeting you here."

"Ben," Reagan breathed, hurrying over to her client, worry etching her brow. "Are you okay?"

"How did you find me?" Ben asked, looking at them both, a surprised expression on his face. "I didn't leave any clues."

"Magic," Greg responded, crossing his arms over his chest. The room was just as nasty as the outside of the place, worn and musty smelling. He hated to even think what kind of things went on in places like this. They were not going to be staying here very long at all.

"Why did you run, Ben?" Reagan asked gently, leading her client over to sit on one of the beds. "You said something about someone trying to kill you?"

Ben sighed and rubbed a hand over his face, looking exhausted. "A hit man is trying to whack me. I barely escaped with my life."

"Why?" Greg asked, ignoring how Ben referred to being killed as whacked. What had he been doing, watching gangster movies or something? "Because of the murder?"

"No," Ben swallowed, looking at Reagan. "Because I know who killed that girl."

Reagan looked over at Greg, surprise in her eyes. He felt the same way. This was epic for their case, but also a dangerous slope depending on who Ben gave up as the killer. "Who was it?" he asked gently, needing to know.

The Handsome Enemy

Ben shook his head, tears glistening in his eyes. "Oh god, I'm so dead. You are too if I tell you. I don't want to die! Just let me leave!"

Reagan laid a hand on his shoulder, concern on her face now. "We are here to help you, Ben. Whoever it was will go to prison, I can promise you that. But you have to tell us who it was. It's the only way I can help."

Ben wiped at his eyes, looking at Greg. He could see the indecision in the young man's eyes. Whoever it was, was scaring the shit out of him. In the recesses of his mind, Greg already had a very short list of who it could be to make Ben react the way he did. He just hoped he was wrong or they were all in some deep shit.

"It's my father," Ben finally said, hanging his head. "He killed her."

Damn. Greg wiped a hand over his face, the absolute worst news they could get now out in the open and one of the names on his mental short list. Now the attempts on Reagan's life made sense. The senator wanted it all to disappear, including them. He had a lot to lose if something like this got out.

"Your father?" Reagan echoed, shock in her voice. Clearly, she hadn't thought of that angle before. "But why? How did you find out?"

The Handsome Enemy

Ben stood, pacing the floor in front of the bed. "I overheard him and someone on the phone discussing it the night before the interview. He sounded agitated and worried about you finding out since you were sniffing around the case. I think you rattled him, Ms. Lister." Ben then drew in a breath, his eyes on the floor beneath his feet. "He saw me before I could get away and I locked myself in the cottage. I wasn't stupid enough to think he was going to let me get away with knowing that he had actually done the killing and started packing my shit so I could get the hell out of dodge. H-he sent someone that night." Ben stopped and looked up at them, a wry smile on his face. "He would kill his own kid just to save his position and his ass. He would sacrifice my freedom to keep his slate clean. I still can't believe it."

"Why did he kill her?" Reagan asked as Ben resumed his pacing, growing more agitated now that the secret was out. Greg was more concerned about their safety than learning the details, but Reagan seemed to need to know so he kept his mouth shut for now.

"I don't know," Ben said, with a shrug. "I didn't even know her that well and I don't suspect he did either. They didn't run in the same circles. I have no idea how she would get tangled up with my father, but it killed her in the long run. Oh god, he is going to kill me. I won't survive this."

The Handsome Enemy

Greg couldn't help but agree. A senator with this kind of black mark on his person was a ticking time bomb. They all were in danger. "We have got to get out of here," he said urgently. "We have to get Ben to safety."

"We have to call Martin," Reagan said, rising from the bed. "He should know about this."

Greg shook his head. While he knew they should tell Martin, the priority was finding somewhere safe to bunker down first.

Chapter 9

Reagan was flabbergasted. The senator killed the woman, not Ben. It still seemed too odd to be true.

"We need to get out of here," Greg was saying. "Get your things, Ben."

She looked at Greg, seeing the tightness in his expression, and inwardly shuddered. They had just stepped into a major issue, one that could get them killed. Now it all was making sense. The knife attack, the chase yesterday, the senator was trying to kill them. He thought she knew that he was involved with the killing way before she actually found out from Ben. "What are we going to do?" she whispered, not wanting to spook Ben.

"We'll figure out something," he whispered back, his eyes on her. "Do you trust me, Reagan?"

Reagan swallowed. Did she trust him? She barely knew him! But he hadn't given her any reason not to trust him and honestly, she had no idea what to do now. The senator had so much more at his disposal and they had to keep Ben alive. He was the only person that was going to be able to bring down his father when the time came. "I-I trust you," she forced out.

He reached over and squeezed her shoulder before looking over at Ben. "Are you ready?"

Ben had a duffel bag slung over his shoulder. He looked utterly exhausted and scared. "I am."

"Good," Greg announced, opening the door. "Let's go before someone catches on. Do you have another car here? We can't continue to be seen in this car."

"I brought the Corvette," Ben said sheepishly, pointing to the sporty car parked around the side of the building. "Not exactly the best one to pick." Reagan groaned. Of all the cars that Ben could pick to hide from his father, he had to pick the flashiest one.

Greg shoved a hand through his hair, looking at Reagan's car. "We can't continue to drive this car. Someone has flagged this car and every moment we drive it, we are easy targets for those who are trying to kill us."

Reagan threw up her hands, looking at him. "Do you have another car in mind then?" The Corvette wouldn't fit all three of them and she didn't see anything for miles except a lonely road with very little traffic coming. They were sitting ducks in the open and even she knew that was not good.

Greg sighed. "Just get in. We will figure it out."

Reagan pursed her lips and climbed in the passenger seat, Ben taking the back seat as Greg climbed in and fired up the car. "Is there any place we can go?" he asked softly. "Any place that very few people know about?"

Reagan thought for a moment, shaking her head. "No. We just need to go to a hotel or something."

"We can go to my mom's cabin," Ben offered up. "Dad doesn't even know about that place. It's not far from the city but far enough to keep us out of it for now."

Greg dropped the car into reverse and Reagan looked back at Ben, giving him an encouraging smile. "Lead the way."

***

The cabin was at the end of a long road toward upstate New York, the nearest neighbor a mile down the road. Reagan climbed out of the car and looked around. She could hear only the sounds of nature. After a lifetime in the city, it was a bit nerve-wracking.

"Come on," Ben said, motioning to them as he walked up to the front porch. "The key is just above the doorframe." After locating the key, he opened the door and disappeared through the doorway.

Greg grabbed Reagan's arm and pulled her back, away from the door. "This is some serious shit," he said urgently, looking at her. Reagan nodded, knowing exactly what he was talking about. The senator was in political office and if Ben was lying about this and they went to the police, it could be their careers if not their lives. "How sure are you that he is telling the truth?"

Reagan looked at the real concern in Greg's eyes, knowing it reflected in hers as well. "I-I'm not sure," she admitted, wanting nothing more than to get in her car and flee. "I never thought he killed that woman, but his father? What is the motivation? Why would a senator take such a risk?"

Greg shook his head. "I don't know but this changes the game, Reagan."

Reagan nodded and he released her arm. With a senator involved, they would have to be very careful who they trusted until everything could be sorted out. "No cell phones right now," Greg said as they walked toward the cabin. "I don't want to run the risk of being tracked. We don't know what the senator is doing."

"Agreed," she said as they entered. It was a modest cabin, with cheery furniture and plenty of firewood for the large fireplace that dominated one wall. Ben was at the fridge, a beer in his hand as Greg secured the door, propping a chair under the knob for good measure.

"There are two bedrooms," Ben said as Reagan looked around. "Mom keeps the fridge and cabinets stocked so we have plenty of food."

"That's good, Ben," Greg said, leaning against the door. "Do you have any proof that your father did this?"

Reagan watched as Ben shook his head, staring at the beer bottle. "No, I don't. I know it's hard to believe that my dad would do something so heinous, but he did. I heard him say as much. He killed her and all this time I thought he was helping me out when all he was attempting to do was to save his own hide."

Reagan still couldn't totally believe her client. As much as she wanted to, she needed proof. No one was going to believe them without proof.

"I'm going to crash," Ben said, throwing his bottle into the trash. "I need some sleep."

She nodded absently waiting until he had closed the bedroom door before looking up at Greg. "What's the plan?" she asked.

Greg's expression was inscrutable. "I really don't know," he answered. "I wish I had a thought, but honestly I don't."

Reagan sighed. She didn't have a clue what to do either. They were not in a good place with this new revelation. Greg pushed away from the door and headed toward her, stopping mere inches away from her, his eyes searching hers. "I won't let anyone hurt you," he said urgently, reaching out to grip her upper arms. "You can trust me, Reagan."

She looked at him, worry churning in her gut. "I know," she answered. "But it doesn't make it any better."

He looked as if he wanted to say something before his lips descended on hers. As the initial shock of him kissing her wore off, it was replaced with something that ignited a fire low in her belly. Her hands landed on his chest as he deepened their kiss, his hands sliding down her arms and gripping her hips, pulling her close. She slid her own hands up his chest and encircled his neck, her hands delving in his hair. A growl came out from one of them, which one she wasn't sure. Her body was on fire, the need to just simply be in his arms stronger than Reagan could have imagined.

"Reagan," he whispered against her lips, nipping at her lower lip with his teeth. Reagan moaned, for that was about all she could do, clinging to him like she was drowning. She was drowning, in feelings and emotions she was very unsure of.

With great reluctance, she pulled out of his arms, the taste of him still on her lips. "I'm sorry," he said quietly as she struggled to compose herself. "I just had to kiss you."

Reagan forced out a ragged breath. "We can't complicate things with, with this." Their lives were in danger right now and she was kissing Greg. This was not the time nor the place to be considering a relationship, sexual or otherwise.

Greg nodded and turned away, removing the chair from the door before walking outside, closing the door behind him. Reagan sank onto the chair in the living room, her knees a little wobbly from the searing kiss. The last time she had kissed a guy was well over two years ago, a brief fling with a man that was in her apartment building. He was on a traveling assignment with his company and they had fun together, but once the initial physical desire had been sated, the entire thing had fizzled out. When his contract was up, she didn't bother to pretend like she was going to contact him again. But this thing with Greg, her blood was nearly sizzling in her veins to touch him again, to have him kiss her like there was no tomorrow. It was frightening and strangely exciting at the same time.

Her phone vibrated in her pocket and Reagan pulled it out, seeing Martin's name flash on the screen. She shouldn't answer it. Greg had said no phones and he was right, given the way his associate had been able to track Ben's earlier. He had told her that they couldn't trust anyone else and she believed him. This was a dangerous game, a game that she was afraid they wouldn't be able to win.

Chapter 10

Greg took a deep breath inward and let it out, his body still on fire from the kiss he had just shared with Reagan. Why he had kissed her, he didn't know, but it had seemed like a good idea at the time. At least she hadn't hauled off and hit him or something and based on her reaction, she seemed to enjoy it just as much as he did. She was right though; they couldn't add another level of complication on top of what they were already dealing with. There would be plenty of time to sort out feelings and whatnot after they got through this.

Looking up at the sky, Greg tried to figure out their next step. This was crazy. A senator, involved with a murder? It was like a TV drama. Except this time there were real lives and careers involved. If Ben was wrong about this, both he and Reagan were screwed. Even if they escaped with their lives, their careers would be over and with the senator as an enemy, he would be lucky to get a job flipping burgers. But if Ben was right, well, that was another inherent risk in itself. And now he had to protect both him and Reagan. He wouldn't let her get hurt.

Greg ran a hand down his face, feeling the weariness start to set in from lack of sleep. Reagan was an amazing woman, one that was intriguing for any man.

She was honest, strong, and didn't lack the drive to snap back, all of which he could appreciate. And that kiss, hell, it was the best one he had experienced in quite a while. His last relationship was a few years ago, dating another lawyer who could understand the late nights and frustration of the job. But even that relationship paled in comparison to the searing heat that he had just generated with Reagan over this one kiss. "You're complicating things, Greg," he muttered to himself, looking back at the cabin. No proof, Ben had no proof of his father's involvement other than he owned the penthouse. Without proof, they were taking a huge risk.

His phone vibrated and he pulled it out of his pocket, seeing Martin's number flashing on the screen. While they probably needed to touch base with the boss, Greg couldn't take the risk in doing so. If the senator was involved in this murder and cover-up, then anyone could have tapped their phones. Or they could draw the coordinates off the cell towers if he were to answer the phone. Martin was going to be pissed, but what could he do? He tucked the phone back into his pocket and walked around the perimeter of the cabin, checking to see what kinds of paths and hiding places were available. The cabin was pretty remote, but not remote enough, though there was nothing he could do about the safety right now. They would have to keep their eyes and ears open tonight to ensure that no one had gotten on their trail.

Taking in a deep breath, he walked back inside the cabin, finding Reagan rooting around in the kitchen, a bloom of red on her face as their eyes met. "I figured I would find us something to eat," she said nervously, wiping her hands on her skirt. "I think there's enough things here to fix spaghetti."

"That would be good," he answered, leaning against the counter. "Do you know how to fix spaghetti?"

She nodded, finding a pan to dump the sauce and a bag of frozen meatballs in. "It won't be homemade but it will be hot and will fill us up."

"I can't complain about that," Greg answered. "Hey Reagan, about that kiss."

She held up her hand, cutting him off. "Hey, we are both adults that got caught up in a moment. I believe we can be professionals still."

"I was going to say that I don't regret it," he said slowly, grinning as he heard her carefully planned speech. "But if you want to go that route, well, I can't say that it won't happen again."

"It can't happen again," she blurted out. "We are running from someone that wants to kill not only my client but now us. We have more important things to worry about than a kiss."

He chuckled and let her have the last word for now. She could deny it all she wanted to, but he had felt the fire, passion, and need when they kissed. Once this was all over, they would talk about this between them.

***

Ben didn't come out for supper. Reagan knocked on the door once or twice, but got no answer and just left him alone. She and Greg ate in silence, the only sound of the night all around the cabin. "So," Greg said as they picked up their plates and took them to the sink. "What's the plan now?"

She sighed and rinsed off their plates. "I don't know really." She had no idea what to do. This was far beyond what she was used to dealing with. "What would you do?"

Greg shrugged, leaning against the counter. "I really don't know either. I'm going to be honest and not pretend that I can fix this. I'm just as stumped as you are."

Reagan sighed, wiping her hands on the kitchen towel. She had hoped he had come up with a grand plan, though if he was anything like her, all he had thought about was that kiss they had shared. She hated to think of it constantly, but it was hard not to. Even in the face of a very dangerous situation, Reagan could still feel the weight of his lips against hers.

Ben's door finally opened and he emerged, his phone in his hand. "My dad called," he said as they both stared at him. "I-I answered it."

"Shit," Greg swore. "Why did you do that?"

"I-I'm sorry," Ben responded, looking pale. "I didn't think about it until I heard his voice."

Reagan walked to Ben and grabbed the phone out of his hand, attempting not to lose her temper with her client. "It's okay, Ben."

"No it's not," Greg muttered. Reagan shot him a look as she set the phone on the counter and pointed to the food still on the stove. "Get something to eat and we will figure out our next step."

Ben walked to the stove and Reagan crossed the room to stand near Greg, worry on her face. "What do we do?" she hissed. A used cell phone meant they could be tracked.

Greg crossed over to the phone, threw it on the floor, and smashed it under his shoe.

"What are you doing?" Reagan asked as she watched him destroy the phone. Ben had already made the call. The damage was done.

Greg looked up at her, his expression angry. "I don't know. I felt like I needed to destroy something."

Reagan hugged her midsection with her arms, her mind in a whirlwind of thoughts. They were now exposed to the senator. If she were a betting woman, she figured they had less than an hour to try and figure out something to keep them all alive. "What do we do?" she asked softly as Ben finished his food.

"I don't know," Greg said softly right before the lights went out. Reagan didn't even have time to react before Greg pushed her to the floor, covering her body with his for protection. "Stay down," he said urgently. "If we can stay low, we might get out of this. If we don't, they will shoot us."

"Oh god," she breathed, her heart hammering in her chest. "Ben."

"I'll take care of him," Greg said softly, touching her face briefly. Reagan wanted to beg him to stay, to close her eyes and wish all of this away, but she couldn't. This was real life and she was scared to death.

Greg climbed off her and she rolled onto her stomach on the wooden floor, sliding her body over to the couch as she waited for the next step. As she raised herself up just enough to glimpse the curtained window, a shadow crossed over the space, silhouetted by the moonlight. Reagan bit her lip to keep from crying out. Someone was really out there. This was not just a power outage, not that she had thought it was to begin with.

"Hey," Greg's voice breathed by her ear. "We are going out the back. Ben's right behind me."

"OK," she whispered, but then the window shattered.

Reagan was pushed back to the floor roughly, bruising her knees and momentarily stunning her. Someone's body covered hers, not the familiar warmth of Greg's from earlier. "Stay down," Ben's shaky voice said softly in her ear.

"Where's Greg?" she asked in a hushed tone. She couldn't see her hand in front of her face at the moment and Ben was pushing her into the floor with his body weight. Greg had just been right beside them. So where was he now? She wanted him beside her. She heard a loud crash from behind, almost like someone had fallen hard into the wall. Reagan pushed Ben away from her body to look in the direction of the sound. Two men fought in the shaft of moonlight streaming through the broken window, their identities obscured by the inky darkness. Reagan gasped as she saw the flash of a knife, her heart in her throat. One of those shadows was Greg, but she had no idea which one.

"Come on," Ben urged, tugging at her arm. "We have got to get out of here."

The Handsome Enemy

"We can't leave Greg," she stated, trying to figure out what she needed to do. How could she help him when she didn't even know which one he was?

The two men crashed into the side table near the fireplace and for a brief second, she saw Greg's features, making up her mind that she had to help out. Fumbling against the table, her hands wrapped around the base of the lamp that was there, yanking it hard to get the cord from the outlet. "What are you doing?" Ben hissed as she rose from her position on the floor and hurled herself at the men, hitting the one that she thought was not Greg. If it was him, she and Ben were dead.

The man grunted as she whacked him in the back and he went down at her feet before she whacked him again, doling out her frustration on his back.

Hands gripped her waist and pulled her back. "Hey it's okay. He's not getting up."

Reagan turned and fell into Greg's arms, a sob escaping her throat. "Oh, thank god that's not you."

"I'm pretty glad it isn't either," he chuckled as he wrapped his arms around her. She dropped the lamp and held onto him for dear life, so glad that he was okay. They were okay. Greg winced and she drew back, her hand coming back with something warm and sticky. "Are you okay? Where, what?"

"I'm fine," he grunted as light flared in the room.

Reagan turned to see Ben holding a candle, his face ghostly white in the light. "I found this."

She turned her attention back to Greg. There was blood all over the front of his shirt. "Where are you bleeding?" she asked, her voice trembling as she started feeling him all over.

"If I had known this would get your hands on me like this, I would have gotten stabbed sooner," he joked as her hands ran over his shoulders. "Shit, that hurt."

Reagan ignored his smart comment and found the tear in his shirt, feeling more stickiness. "You are cut on your shoulder," she stated, not allowing the hysteria to rise in her throat just yet.

"I was stabbed in the shoulder," he corrected her as Ben brought the light closer. "There's a slight difference."

"S-stabbed?" Reagan stammered, feeling a bit lightheaded. Greg gripped her tightly and steered her toward the couch, forcing her to sit. "Ben, go find some more candles, will you?"

Ben took off running as Reagan gripped Greg's hand, worried that he was going to die. He couldn't die. "We've got to look at your wound," she said, standing. She had to be strong for the both of them, take charge of the situation. "Sit."

Greg gave her a look, but she pointed at the couch, bringing the candle that Ben had left on the coffee table closer. "Are you sure there's just one of them?" she asked, biting her lip as she saw the blood.

"If there wasn't, we would be dead by now," Greg said, looking over at the body lying on the floor. "You saved my life."

"You were trying to save mine," Reagan answered. "Can you get your shirt off?"

"I've never been asked if I could get undressed in front of a beautiful woman before," he answered, groaning as he pulled the shirt over his head. The wound was pretty deep, positioned right beside his shoulder blade. Reagan grabbed the discarded shirt and pressed it against the wound.

"How bad is it, doc?" Greg asked softly as Reagan dabbed at the blood that seemed to be everywhere on his back now.

"It's not bad," she lied as she looked at the jagged wound. "I think I can glue it back together."

"I'm glad you are a lawyer and not a doctor," he chuckled.

Reagan bit her lip and wiped away the blood. "We need to clean it out."

Greg turned toward her, his eyes glazed with pain. "It will be fine, Reagan. Just cover it up."

The Handsome Enemy

She looked at him, noticing his well-formed chest in the candlelight, a sprinkle of hair on the tanned skin, and felt her heart speed up for an entirely different reason. Now that the excitement of nearly being killed yet again was over, she was seeing Greg in a new light, a different light and it was not what she had expected. Her mouth went dry at the thought of touching him. It had to be the near-death experience, right? Realizing that Greg was waiting for her to respond, she shook out of her thoughts. "Absolutely not. You are in pain. Come on, let me take care of you."

She thought he was going to refuse but after a heavy sigh, he stood and followed her to the bathroom, the candle in his hand. Reagan made him sit on the toilet. She rummaged through the cabinets under the sink until she found some gauze and a half-empty tube of antibiotic cream. "This is probably going to sting," she said softly as she turned on the faucet. Greg tensed as she ran a wet rag over the cut but was quiet through her application of the medication and the bandage. For someone who was not accustomed to pain and danger, she was surprised at how he had handled himself tonight. Greg was not the ordinary lawyer type she had anticipated when she had first met him and what really worried her was the growing attraction she had for the man. He surprised and intrigued her at every turn and Reagan was worried that it might drift into a dangerous zone for her personally.

"All done," she finally said, admiring her handiwork. While she had never bandaged anything past a simple paper cut, she had done pretty decent in getting the bandage to stick on Greg's shoulder.

He stood and rolled his shoulders, clearly in pain as he did it. "We need to phone Martin," he said, turning to face her.

"We need to call the cops," she sighed, throwing the rag in the sink. This was far beyond what she could handle. It was time to let the real heroes in blue take it from here.

"We can't," Greg said roughly, taking the washrag and washing up the blood that was caked on his chest. "Ben will go to jail and if the senator is really behind this, be dead before the morning. Martin's an upstanding guy. He will tell us what we need to do."

"Alright," Reagan answered, not really wanting to make the decision anyway, as she walked to the door.

Greg's hand shot out and grabbed her arm, spinning her around to face him. "Thank you," he said softly as she tried to compute the fact that he was touching her. "For doctoring me up."

"I, you're welcome," she said softly, looking into his eyes. It was scary what she was feeling; a range of emotions dancing around in her body.

Greg leaned over and brushed his lips against hers. The spiral of heat that followed ignited Reagan's blood. While the first kiss had been unexpected, this one was tender, sweeter than she could have imagined. Reagan felt herself lean into the kiss, her hands coming up to grip Greg's shoulders. He winced and drew back from her touch, pain in his eyes.

"I am so sorry," she said, the moment now gone. "I didn't, I forgot."

Greg opened his mouth to say something but a knock at the bathroom door interrupted him. "I got some more candles," Ben announced through the door. "If you need that romantic glow in the bathroom, that is."

Reagan turned and opened the door, finding Ben standing there with a stupid grin on his face, his hands full of candles of various sizes and colors. "Move," she said, embarrassed that not only had she been kissing Greg but also that Ben thought it was more than it had been. The problem was, she would have liked for it to be more. That was what worried her.

Chapter 11

Greg drummed his fingers along the table as he sat and waited for Martin to arrive, his shoulder hurting like hell. After his small interlude with Reagan in the bathroom, she hadn't really talked to him. She had been pacing in the kitchen area after their conference call with Martin. Martin had told them to stay put, that Greg was right in not calling the cops. *"We can't afford for you to be found with a supposed killer who should be in the Hamptons,"* he had said. *"I'll come and get you all and we will get Ben to a safe place."* Greg was surprised that Martin seemed to accept Ben's story about his father being the killer without many questions, though his words had expressed his concern over the senator's involvement. *"This will be extremely high-profile now once the senator is arrested,"* he had told them. *"We will have to be careful on who we trust until then."* He couldn't be more correct. Greg knew that their lives were in extreme danger even now and suspected that the senator already knew that he and Reagan knew the truth. Until he was behind bars, no one was safe.

Lights lit up the front of the cabin and Reagan stopped her pacing, looking nervously at Greg. "It's got to be Martin, right?"

"I'm sure it is," Greg said, looking over at their attempted killer in the corner. The man was now awake, matted blood on his hair where Reagan had struck him with the lamp. They had tied him up while he was still knocked out cold, gagged him and set him in the corner. They were really unsure of what to do with him. Maybe Martin could call the authorities to come get him after the fact.

"It's not anyone for you, is it?" Greg called to him.

The guy glowered at Greg but said nothing, not even a mumble as Greg got up and walked to the door, picking up the trusty lamp in the process for protection. It had worked so well for Reagan that maybe they could patent it when all of this was said and done.

A knock sounded and he opened the door, seeing Martin in the bright car lights. "Nice weapon," the older lawyer remarked casually as he entered through the doorway. "Were you going to brighten me to death?"

"Desperate times, man." Greg shrugged, setting it down on the nearby table.

Reagan walked over and Martin gave her a brief hug, a fatherly look on his face. "Are you okay, my dear?" he asked.

"I-I've been better," she answered. Greg saw the worry and anxiety on her face and longed to comfort her but refrained. Now was not the time nor the place. "But we are alive thanks to Greg."

The Handsome Enemy

Martin looked back at him. "So I guess I should be asking if you are okay."

"I'll live," he responded as Ben came into the living room. "But I'd rather get out of here if you don't mind."

"Sure, come on," Martin motioned. "I have a van out here waiting to transport you all to another location."

Quickly they gathered up their things and blew out the candles. They made sure that the plastic Greg and Ben had hung over the broken window would hold for another day or so until Ben could make some calls and get it fixed. Then they all followed Martin out to the van, which was still idling in the drive.

"What should we do with the guy in the house?" Ben asked as they walked down the steps. "I mean we can't just leave him here."

"I'll make an anonymous call about a break-in," Martin answered as he threw open the door. "Don't worry, I'll take care of it."

Reagan climbed in and Greg followed her, noting that the back of the van didn't have any seating and was void of anything. There were no windows. Ben climbed in and Martin shut the door behind him, enclosing them in the space. Martin climbed into the driver's seat and looked back at them apologetically. "Sorry guys," he said. "This was the only thing I had at the last minute that would keep Ben's identity away from the public eye."

"It's fine," Reagan said, giving him a tired smile. "I'm just glad you came and got us."

He nodded and pulled the van out of the driveway.

Greg stretched out his feet before him and crossed his arms, feeling the pull in his shoulder. The hard ride of the van wasn't going to be nice on his wound and his face was starting to hurt from where the attacker's fists had actually connected. Hell, he was a mess.

Looking over, he saw Reagan watching him, her face pale in the dim light. "Hey," he said. "Are you okay?"

She laughed softly, rubbing her arms with her hands. "No, I'm not. I am going to take a vacation after this trial."

Greg reached over and grasped her hand with his, feeling the slight tremor in her touch. "We are going to be just fine," he stated, though his words seemed hollow even to his own ears. He had no idea if they were going to be okay. She leaned into him and he draped his arm over her shoulder, rubbing her arm with his hand. He could understand her fears, her worries, because he had some himself.

"Where are we going?" Ben asked, his voice soft in the small space.

The Handsome Enemy

Greg shrugged, unable to answer that question. He didn't know Martin all that well, but was assured that he would take them somewhere safe until they could sort all this out. More importantly, they had to figure out how to get Ben to a safe location without the press finding out, or his father, if Ben's words were true. His life would be in danger and Greg didn't know how they would protect him.

The van stopped an hour later, the back door sliding open as Martin climbed out of the driver's seat.

"No, no!" Ben started shrieking, sliding back as far as he could as a figure came into the light.

"Hello Ben," he said with a grin. "Good to see you again."

"Who the hell are you?" Greg asked instantly, a sinking feeling in his stomach. The guy looked like hired muscle, dressed in all black with a wicked-looking scar down the side of his face.

"None of your damn business," the man replied, hiking a thumb over his shoulder. "Get out, now."

"He's the one who tried to kill me!" Ben wailed, shaking all over.

Greg placed an arm against Reagan to hold her back. He stood up to give some height on the guy. "We aren't going anywhere. Where's Martin?"

The Handsome Enemy

The man stepped aside and Martin filled the doorway, a gun in his hand. Greg knew instantly what was going on. "You double-crossed us," he said, hating the fact that he didn't see this coming. Trust no one had been their number one rule, Martin's own words to them, and they had trusted in a person that they never expected to betray them.

"Get out, Greg," Martin was saying, waving the gun in their direction. "And shut the hell up, Ben."

"Martin?" Reagan asked, her face full of confusion. "Why are you doing this?"

Martin sighed, looking agitated. "Reagan, I had such high hopes for you. If only you had just quit the case like I thought you would, you wouldn't have gotten caught up in this mess." He then pointed the gun at Greg. "He was supposed to push you over the edge, to drive you so crazy with his help that you would want to quit to get your own case again, but I don't get that feeling. Actually, I think he has feelings for you. Isn't that right, Greg?"

"You won't get away with this," Greg said as Reagan gasped at Martin's stinging words. "We will bring you to justice."

Martin shook his head, waving the gun back and forth with his hand. "I'm afraid that will not be possible considering you will be dead in an hour or so. It's a shame really. Not only are you both pretty decent lawyers, but also pretty good detectives. Well, maybe not. You didn't see this coming."

He stepped back and the man in all black stepped in, grabbing for Ben first and dragging him out. Ben landed with a thud on the asphalt. He then turned toward them, giving them a look. "I can either drag you out as well or you can come out nice and easy."

Reagan was clutching at Greg's arm, her fear radiating into his body. He knew she was scared, hell, he was too, but they were going to get through this. He was not going to let them die tonight. Quickly Greg assessed the situation, not seeing any other option at this moment. They were going to have to comply. "We will come out," he said darkly, seeing another man dressed in all black step out from around the vehicle. One he could fight, but two, he wouldn't be helping the situation by getting himself beat up by two goons. The man moved aside and they both exited the vehicle, Reagan sliding her hand into his as they did. He gave her hand a squeeze before releasing it, not wanting to show any weakness in front of Martin or anyone else. Worst-case scenario was that they would end up all dead, but he intended to make sure Reagan got out of this alive, even if he didn't.

Chapter 12

Reagan couldn't believe this. Martin was involved? She could feel the cold barrel of the gun pressed in her back as they were marched toward a warehouse in an isolated part of town, a part where no one would hear the gunshots when they happened. A sob caught in the back of her throat and Reagan pressed her hand to her mouth, willing herself not to break down now. She wasn't going to die here tonight.

They walked inside the warehouse and were taken to a small storage room where they were forced to sit on the floor among cleaning and office supplies. After roughly tying their hands and feet together, the goons walked out of the room, leaving only Martin with the gun in his hands. "We will find out what the senator wants to do with you but I can guarantee it's not anything good," he stated, giving Reagan a sad smile. "I really had high hopes for you, my dear, in my firm. It was just a stroke of bad luck that this happened. Believe me when I say I didn't want your life to end up like this."

"Why are you doing this?" she asked, her voice full of emotion. "This isn't you, Martin." She had worked for this man, worked side by side with him and never thought that he could be involved in such a crime.

The Handsome Enemy

"Darling, you would be surprised what you will do to line your pockets full of money," Martin said with a laugh and a wink. "After all, I'm not getting any younger. See you all later."

Ben started to cry softly as the door was closed and they were plunged into darkness, the sound of the door locking a final reminder that they were truly in this situation. This wasn't a dream or a nightmare, this was reality and Reagan had no idea what she was going to do to keep herself alive.

"Don't worry," Greg said softly beside her, inching over until they were side to side, his warmth seeping through the coldness that had settled in her bones. "We will get out of this, Reagan."

"How?" she said, choking on the word. Their situation hadn't gotten any better and now they were locked in a room, awaiting whatever fate the senator had in mind for them. Based on what Martin had alluded to, it wasn't good by any means.

She heard Greg blow out a breath. "Now that I haven't quite figured out."

Reagan laughed, because she literally didn't know what else to do. Even in this type of situation, Greg still could keep his sense of humor.

"Why are you laughing?" Ben said, annoyance in his voice. Apparently, he had quit crying seeing that it wasn't going to get him out of this.

"I don't know," she answered, chuckling. "I guess I should go through all the range of emotions before I'm shot." Maybe they would think she was crazy and let her loose that way.

"We have to think through this logically," Greg said as Reagan's laughter died down. "There are three of us and three of them, right?"

"That we know of," Reagan reminded him.

"Well, those two guys are employed by my father," Ben added. "I've never seen anyone else."

"So no more than three if we exclude the senator," Greg finalized. "We need to get out of here and overtake them before the senator arrives."

"No shit Sherlock," Ben said. Reagan could almost imagine the eye rolling that he was giving Greg in the dark. "How do you suppose we do that?"

"Draw them in," Greg finally said. Reagan thought his plan sucked, but she didn't have any other thoughts so it was going to be the one they would have to go with.

"I need you to untie me," Greg continued, nudging Reagan in the side with his elbow. "I'm going to scoot back and let you work on the knots."

"Okay," she said. After a few attempts, they were able to maneuver themselves into a position where Reagan could reach the knots. She tugged at them until her nails were broken and her fingers were hurting, finally getting one of them to loosen enough to where Greg could slide his hand out. "Thank god," he said, making quick work of the ropes at his feet before relieving Reagan of hers. Reagan rubbed her raw wrists as she heard Greg shuffle over to help Ben get out of his. She patted around the floor to see what they had around them. What she wouldn't give for any kind of light right now!

"So, what next?" she asked.

"I have a candle," Ben said. "I stuck a few in my hoodie pocket for later and forgot they were in there."

"Now all we need is a light," Greg said, excitement in his voice.

A light flared in Ben's direction and she saw the amusement on his face. "I have one of those too."

"I can almost forgive you for getting us in this situation," Reagan replied as Ben handed her one of the lit candles. She held it high over her head, illuminating the rest of the room. There were brooms and mops that could be used as weapons, which was good. They could arm themselves for the next person that came in the door. "We have weapons."

Greg followed her finger to where she was pointing at, a grin splitting his face. "Good. Let's get those and then we can make some noise to get these guys to open the door. Ben, throw a fit."

"Why does it have to be me?" Ben asked, looking hurt.

Greg sighed loudly as Reagan grabbed the brooms and mops, giving them to Greg and Ben. "Because you owe us."

"Fine," Ben grumbled, standing and taking one of the brooms. "But I can't be responsible if they just open up the door and shoot us all."

"It won't matter because we will all be dead then," Reagan muttered as Ben started to beat on the door.

"Let me out! I want to go home!" he yelled.

She and Greg crouched on either side of the door, adrenaline flowing through her veins as they waited for the door to open. If this didn't work, she didn't know what they were going to do. "Whatever happens, run," Greg mouthed to her as Ben's rantings got louder. She nodded, her heart in her throat. This was not an action movie or video game. She could really get killed doing this and Martin could walk free. The senator could walk free. There was no way in hell she was going to allow that to happen. They would have to walk over her dead body.

"Shut the hell up, Ben!" Martin's voice raved through the door as he banged something against it. Ben didn't and only banged louder as the broom

The Handsome Enemy

handle became slippery in Reagan's sweaty palms. Finally, they heard the scrape of a key and Ben froze as the door swung wide open before he bolted out, yelling and swinging.

"What the—?" they heard Martin ask before there was a clatter to the ground as Ben rushed Martin and knocked him over.

"Now! Use whatever you can to attack them!" Greg shouted and charged out of the room. Reagan stood and did the same, wielding her broom like it was a double-edged sword. She knew the broom wasn't the best choice of weapons, but it did have a wooden handle that could be swung hard enough to do some damage. Reagan just hoped she could inflict enough to get them out of here. Martin was on the ground, Ben on top as he wrestled the gun away from the older lawyer. One of the other guys started to charge toward Reagan, anger in his eyes, and Reagan started swinging her broom before the guy went down, Greg standing behind him with his weapon in his hands. He had hit him from behind as the guy had nearly reached Reagan. But he didn't stay down for long. Reagan watched in horror as the guy got back to his feet, turning toward Greg with a thunderous expression on his face. Greg picked up his broken mop and started swinging. Reagan started to charge the guy, wanting to help Greg, but Greg was able to wrestle him to the ground, punching him hard in the face. Reagan thought her heart was going to beat out of her chest as she watched Greg stand. Ben had Martin down on the ground with the other goon nowhere in sight. They had done it. They were going to get out alive.

Greg grabbed her hand and pulled her toward the door. "Come on," he said. "We have to go."

"Don't worry, I'm not complaining about leaving this place," Reagan muttered as she hurried to keep up. They would go to the cops now, no doubt about it. The main door to the warehouse opened as they approached it and Reagan skidded to a stop, nearly running over the senator in the process.

"Well, well," he said, crossing his arms over his chest. "This is interesting."

Chapter 13

Greg pushed Reagan behind him and stared at the senator. He didn't look like he was doing well at all, his normal regal demeanor whittled down to exhaustion on his face and bags under his eyes. "Let us go," he tried.

The senator laughed, a harsh sound to their ears. Behind him was the missing goon, standing in front of their only chance of escape. "Let you go? I'm afraid we are far from that now."

He then motioned to the man that they hadn't seen after their escape. "Get them."

"Nobody move," Ben's voice boomed in the space. They all turned to see Ben holding Martin's gun, a determined look on his face. "You are not getting away with this, Father."

"You son of a bitch," the senator said, his face darkening with anger. "You're my flesh and blood and you dare turn a gun on me?"

"Call the cops," Ben answered, nodding to Reagan as he threw a cell phone her way. "Now."

Reagan fumbled with the phone as Greg kept his eye on the other man, the one who looked like he could spit nails. "You're going to prison for that girl's

The Handsome Enemy

murder," the senator continued. "No one will ever believe you didn't do it."

"Why did you kill her?" Greg asked as Reagan spoke urgently into the phone. "What did she do to you?"

The senator spat on the floor. "She was working one of the parties, overheard some information she shouldn't have. I didn't want to kill her, but what choice did I have?"

"You could have let her go," Ben announced. "And why frame me? I don't understand."

The senator looked directly at his son, his flesh and blood, and sighed. "You should really learn when to take one for your old man. I would have gotten you out of that mess. No senator's son can go to prison!"

Ben's hand shook as he kept the gun pointed at his father. "And no father should frame his own child." The explosion came out of nowhere as Greg pushed Reagan down on the floor, covering her with his body. It was then that he realized the sound had been the gun firing.

Looking up, Greg saw the crimson stain spread along the front of the senator's shirt, a look of surprise on his face as he looked at his son. "You shot me."

"Goodbye, Father," Ben said softly, pointing the gun at the remaining goon who had a surprised expression on his face. Clearly, he hadn't imagined Ben would shoot his father nor was he willing to take a bullet for the senator. "I suggest you run," Ben said.

The goon didn't even stop to think and ran out the door as the wail of police sirens filled the air. Greg scrambled off Reagan and helped her up off the floor as Ben dropped the gun, his expression stone-cold. The senator fell to his knees, his eyes widening before he collapsed on the floor. Greg hurried over and checked for a pulse, finding none. The senator was dead, killed by his son, the last person he had expected. "Is he dead?" Ben asked, no emotion in his voice. Greg looked back and nodded as Reagan brought her hand up to her mouth. "Good," Ben answered, looking at his father's body, his expression passive.

Greg looked over at Reagan and she nodded, shock on her face. She didn't believe that this would have been the outcome either. Whatever had just happened, the bigger thought was that their ordeal was over. They had survived.

"Freeze!"

Greg turned to see a couple of uniformed police officers in the doorway, their guns trained on them. "Get down on the ground!"

He wasted no time doing just that, turning his head so he could see Reagan at all times. She too had complied, worry in her eyes as the police officer checked the senator's neck for a pulse. "We will be just fine," he whispered to her, hoping that she had gotten the message as he was hauled to his feet, his hands behind his back. They were going to be just fine.

***

The next hours were hellacious. After the police arrived, it took a good while to figure out what had happened. Greg and Reagan were separated and escorted to police cars before being taken to the station for endless rounds of questioning. Greg, after having a cup of coffee and answering every question about their adventure and the senator's death for hours, was released. Ben had apparently given the police all that they needed to know in terms of a confession, telling them that he had shot his father. Martin had sung like a canary when pressed, according to the detective that had interviewed Greg, and had confessed that it had been the senator that had killed the woman, not Ben. From what Greg could gather, Ben would be formally charged with his father's death but based on Greg's and Reagan's testimony, would be cleared from the waitress's death. It had been a bitter price to pay.

Greg walked out of the police station, his hands in his pockets, and spied Reagan near the street, her arms wrapped around her midsection. "Hey," he said softly. She turned and he could see the tearstains on her cheeks. "Are you okay?"

She shook her head. "I'll never be okay. Martin was my mentor, the man I looked up to. I-I still can't believe he was involved in this."

"Money makes people do crazy things," Greg admitted, surprised himself that Martin had been involved. The senator, well he wasn't completely surprised, but Martin had fooled them all. "It's not your fault."

"I know," she said softly, looking up at him. He could see the anger and regret in her eyes, knowing exactly how she felt. He was angered at the entire situation, hated the fact that Ben was put in a position that would cost him his freedom in the long run. If only the senator had not pinned this on his son in the first place, Ben could still be part of the free world. Now he was looking at up to fifteen years in prison. "So what's next?" she asked, her eyes searching his. "What are your plans?"

Greg stepped forward, his hands gently gripping her upper arms. Suddenly he felt tongue-tied, not sure of himself for the first time in a long while. He had a thought, he just didn't know if he wanted to execute it. Her eyes widened and her lips parted, her breathing shallow much like his was. Did he dare take that leap? Did he dare think there was something more between them than this bizarre case? "Reagan, I ..."

She stepped out of his grasp, looking flustered. "I, um, I can't say that this has been a pleasant experience, Greg."

"That's an understatement," he replied softly, looking at her.

Reagan looked up, giving him a slight smile. "But I can say that if you had not been here, I wouldn't be standing here, still living."

Greg looked at Reagan, thinking that she had done more than just save his life. She had stolen his heart. "I love you," he blurted out.

Reagan's eyes widened. "W-what?"

Greg stepped forward once more, taking her back into his arms. "I love you," he said tenderly. "I don't know when it happened but I know that I can't imagine living my life without you, Reagan."

"Greg," she breathed. "I love you too."

His chest expanded and he released the breath he had been holding. She loved him. "Thank god," he said, gathering her against his chest. "I think I fell in love with you the day you stepped in that elevator."

"You mean that day I tried to break my neck?" she asked, clinging to him.

Greg grinned. "Yes," he said softly. "That day." He pressed a kiss in her hair and then pulled away reluctantly. "Come on, let's get out of here."

Chapter 14

Two Months Later

Reagan sat next to Greg in the courtroom, her hand clasped tightly in his as they watched Martin stand to receive his sentence for his involvement in the mess that had consumed their lives and brought them together. Greg had given up his practice in Texas and moved in with Reagan for the time being. Right now, they both were out of a job with the firm shutting down after Martin's confession. But they had needed this time off to recuperate from their ordeal and decide what to do about their future.

"Martin Fitz," the judge started. "You have pled guilty to the charges presented to you. For your involvement in this heinous act, you will serve fifteen years without the possibility of parole." Reagan watched as her former boss's shoulders slumped, knowing that fifteen years at Martin's age was nearly a life sentence to begin with. He might never taste freedom again. Ben had gotten off rather lightly considering he had shot a senator. Coupled with Martin's confession and both Reagan's and Greg's testimony, Ben would be considered for parole after serving seven years. Reagan was comforted in the fact that they hadn't thrown the book at Ben and that he would get a chance to live his life out from under his father's thumb.

The court adjourned and they walked out together, ignoring the news media as they hailed a cab. Ever since word got out about the senator's death, the media had hounded them for a story. Reagan wanted to move past this part of her life and to her future with Greg. That's all that mattered now. She could feel the weight of the ordeal and the aftermath starting to lift from her shoulders, finally giving her space to breathe now. Life could get back to normal.

"I'm glad that's over with," Greg remarked as the cab pulled up to their apartment building. "Now maybe the media will leave us alone and go find something else to report on."

"I hope so," Reagan echoed as they rode the elevator up to their apartment, glad to be home. And it felt like home with Greg here now. She had never known she could love someone as much as she loved him. Greg shut the door behind them and grabbed her by the waist, pressing a kiss on her lips. "Now I can do this."

"What?" Reagan asked, her mouth forming an O as Greg bent down on one knee in front of her, holding up a dazzling ring nestled in a velvet box.

"I love you, Reagan," he said, giving her a tender smile. "I know it hasn't been a long time since we have known each other, but I can't imagine ever not having you by my side. Will you marry me?"

Reagan's eyes filled with tears as she nodded and Greg rose, sliding the ring on her finger before gathering her in his arms. "I love you," she sobbed, clinging to his shirt.

He kissed her hair and then pulled back to brush his lips over hers. "We will have a long engagement if you want. I know this is all really sudden."

Reagan reached up and placed a finger on his lips. "Love is never sudden. I don't want a long engagement, Greg. I want to be your wife."

He smiled and drew her into a long kiss, one that had them both panting for air afterward. "Take me to bed," Reagan said, reaching for his hand.

Greg nodded and led her to their bedroom. He slowly took off her clothes until she was naked before him. "Beautiful," he said as she reached for his clothes, doing the same to him. Reagan stepped into his arms, their bodies fitting together like they were made for each other. Greg framed her face with his hands, his thumbs stroking her cheeks. "I love you," he said pressing his lips against hers. "So much."

"I love you too," she answered, her hands roaming over his broad shoulders. Greg's hands slid from her face and he spun her around to the bed, lowering them both until he was on top of her. She moaned against his touch, clutching at his shoulders to get him to hurry. She needed him so much.

"You are killing me," Greg said with a growl as he positioned himself above her.

"Please," she begged. He lowered himself in her and Reagan rose up to meet him, reveling in the way he felt. She would never grow tired of this. Greg stifled a groan as he started to move within her, Reagan clutching at his arms, her legs wrapped around him to urge him on. When the orgasm hit her, Reagan cried out, the waves of passion taking over. Greg's moves became frenzied before he joined her, his body stiffening before collapsing on top of her. Reagan moved one of her hands into his hair, stroking it lightly as she felt the aftereffects of their lovemaking. She couldn't live without him. The sunlight caught the diamond and she smiled. He had surprised her yet again as he had been doing since the moment they met. Now that the ordeal was truly over, they could move on with not only their lives, but also their careers. Maybe they would open up a private investigator firm together. The thought made her giggle and Greg rose up, looking at her with an amused expression on his face. "What's so funny?" he asked.

"I was thinking," Reagan answered, giving him a grin, "that we should look into our own private investigator firm."

"Really?" he asked, surprised. "What about being a lawyer?"

"Oh, we could offer those services too," she answered, the plan really starting to form in her mind.

Greg chuckled and rose from the bed, pushing her over to her side of the bed so he could climb in. Reagan immediately went to his side, sighing in contentment when he wrapped an arm around her. "You know, I kind of like the idea," he mumbled into her ear. "But can we talk about it after some sleep?"

Epilogue

Six Months Later

Reagan walked down the aisle, tears in her eyes as she saw Greg waiting at the altar. All their planning was finally coming together and in a few short moments they would be man and wife. It seemed like they had waited an eternity for this day to come and she could not be happier. The quaint little church on the outskirts of the city was a perfect venue and now was packed with their family and friends who would witness the happy nuptials. Even their honeymoon was planned out, a week in Tahiti, with nothing but sand and sunshine. Reagan could not wait.

She reached Greg and he took her hand, turning toward the officiant as he started the ceremony. After her initial thoughts about a PI firm, Greg had really run with it, finding a small space downtown that they could start taking clients. Business was booming and Greg had just recruited a third private investigator to handle the workload. Reagan was loving the fact that she and Greg got to work side by side in the career that they both loved as a team. Life really couldn't be any better.

"Now it's time for the couple to speak their vows," the officiant said, turning to Reagan. "Ladies first."

The Handsome Enemy

Reagan cleared her throat, the words playing in her head like a broken record. She had practiced them enough. "Greg, I take you as my lawfully wedded husband. I promise to never cause you to lose your faith or your trust in me, to always be by your side, and to never make you sleep on a chaise lounge ever again." Greg burst out into laughter, his eyes tearing up. Reagan gave him a cheeky grin and turned to the officiant, who then prompted Greg.

"I, Greg, take you, Reagan, as my lawfully wedded wife," he started out. "I promise to never forsake you or lie to you. I promise to give you whatever I have to make you happy beyond your wildest dreams and to teach you how to be a quiet private investigator." Reagan laughed then, thinking of how he hated how much she talked when they were on a stakeout together. She couldn't help it. Stakeouts were often really boring. "I also promise to love and cherish you for the rest of my days."

Reagan mouthed "I love you" to Greg, her eyes filling with tears. He gave her a wink as the officiant continued, his eyes on hers. She saw love there, trust and affection, all the things she would have hoped to see in her soon-to-be husband. It was funny how life had worked out for them both and she couldn't wait to see what was in store for the future.

The End

What to read next?

If you liked this book, you will also like *The Weekend Girlfriend*. Another interesting book is *Two Reasons to Be Single*.

The Weekend Girlfriend

Jessica has worked hard to be the paralegal that hotshot, sexy attorney Kyle needs. Unfortunately he doesn't see her as just his paralegal but also his own personal assistant. When he blames her for a mix-up in his personal life, Jessica sees no other option but to quit, thinking that her time with him is over. Much to her surprise, Kyle makes a proposition to her that she never thought she would hear coming from his lips. He needs a temporary girlfriend for his sister's wedding and he wants her to be that person. Jessica accepts the challenge and finds herself thrown into his world, learning things about him she never knew. The more time she spends with him outside of work, the more she is drawn to Kyle. As the wedding draws near, she finds herself fighting off some strong feelings for the man. When the wedding weekend is over, will Jessica be able to walk away from Kyle with her heart intact?

Two Reasons to Be Single

Olivia Parker has a job doing what she loves, a wonderful family and plenty of friends, but no luck in the love department. Tired of worrying about it, she decides to swear off love completely and focus on all the good things in her life. Just as she makes her firm resolution, Jake Harper arrives in town and knocks her plans into a tailspin. As the excited single ladies of Morning Glory surround the extremely attractive newcomer, Olivia steers clear of the "casserole brigade," as she calls the women, and tries to keep her distance from Jake. Instead, a variety of situations throw them together and they get to know each other better. They both have reasons for not wanting to get involved in a relationship, but the chemistry between them ignites, even as they desperately attempt to keep it at bay. As things heat up between Olivia and Jake, there is an aura of mystery about him that leaves Olivia certain that he is hiding something. When Jake disappears for a few days without telling Olivia that he is going out of town, she hates the way it makes her feel, and it reminds her of why she was giving up on dating in the first place. As Olivia's feelings for Jake grow, so does the need to find out what exactly brought him to Morning Glory and what he's been hiding.

About Emily Walters

Emily Walters lives in California with her beloved husband, three daughters, and two dogs. She began writing after high school, but it took her ten long years of writing for newspapers and magazines until she realized that fiction is her real passion. Emily likes to create a mental movie in her reader's mind about charismatic characters, their passionate relationships and interesting adventures. When she isn't writing romantic stories, she can be found reading a fiction book, jogging, or traveling with her family. She loves Starbucks, Matt Damon and Argentinian tango.

One Last Thing…

If you believe that *The Handsome Enemy* is worth sharing, would you spend a minute to let your friends know about it?

If this book lets them have a great time, they will be enormously grateful to you – as will I.

Emily

www.EmilyWaltersBooks.com

Manufactured by Amazon.ca
Bolton, ON